Wish
UPON A
Stray

Wish UPON A Stray

YAMILE SAIED MÉNDEZ

SCHOLASTIC INC.

ISBN 978-1-338-68466-7

10 9 8 7 6 5 4 3 2 1   21 22 23 24 25

Printed in the U.S.A.   40
First printing 2021

Book design by Yaffa Jaskoll and Jennifer Rinaldi

To **OLIVIA VALCARCE**, a la patria,
a más libros juntas, a nosotras.

Para mi ahijado, **GIULLIANO SAIED**,
con mucho amor.

CHAPTER 1

"Well done, María Emilia!" said Mrs. Prescott as she placed a corrected test on my desk. Though her voice was soft, I was sure the rest of the class had heard her too.

My cheeks burned, feeling like they were the exact same color as the red *10/10* on the corner of the paper. "For real?"

"Why are you so surprised?" she said, her blues eyes sparkling. "I expected nothing but the best from you." She beamed at me and continued handing out papers to the rest of the class.

Surprised? I was relieved! The feeling was so intense that the whispers of a song started blooming in my heart.

I wanted to sing. I wanted to dance. But my life was not a musical, so instead, I wrote down the beginning of a verse in the lined pages of my notebook.

The mountain's hard to climb, when you think you're all alone . . .

Surprisingly, the lyrics came to me in English. But then, this English practice test had consumed my life for weeks. I hadn't wanted to let my family down. And all my hard work had paid off. When finals arrived in November, less than three months from now, I'd definitely be ready to move on to the next level of English class.

I couldn't wait to tell my parents and Lela, my grandma. Last night, she'd had a dream that we'd be celebrating something today.

Lela's dreams always came true in one way or another.

"Psst!" Violeta, my cousin, called to me from the other side of the room.

When I read the question on her pretty face, I gave her two thumbs-up, joy spilling from me. She smiled back, but her hazel eyes were watery.

"How did *you* do?" I mouthed at her.

She shrugged, and my victory song died down with a sad twang.

Violeta . . .

Violeta and I were the only seventh graders in this after-school English class at the American Institute in downtown Mendoza. While the rest of our friends spent their free hours hanging out at the park, she and I studied for hours. After school. During the weekends. She knew the verbs and vocabulary just as well as I did. And if I was being honest, her English accent was a teensy bit better than mine. Okay, a lot better.

What had happened?

I tried to send her a reassuring smile, but Mrs. Prescott was already back at her desk. "Overall, I'm satisfied with your grades," she said.

Around me, most of the kids smiled.

My heart gave a little gallop when Nahuel caught my eye and winked. With his black hair that swooped over his large brown eyes, he was the cutest boy in class. Although he was only a couple of months older than me, he was already in the first year of high school, which in Argentina starts in eighth grade.

Before he saw me blush red as a beet, I turned back toward Mrs. Prescott.

"The scores in the written section were good, mostly," she said. Maybe it was my imagination, but I thought her eyes flitted to Violeta. "Still, I feel most of you aren't quite ready for the listening comprehension and conversational parts of the final tests. I need all of you to practice with someone who's fluent in English or with each other any time you can."

Violeta and I could practice with my parents, who spoke English, but what about the rest of the class?

As if she'd read my mind, Mrs. Prescott added, "There's a lot of technology at your fingertips, kids. Use your noggins."

The class laughed. Mrs. Prescott was a proper English lady, straight from London, but every once in a while, she threw in random slang words in the best American accent ever.

Decades ago, when she was young, she'd come to Mendoza on a tour of the world-class wineries in the valley and had fallen in love with not only the place but also the tour guide. They'd gotten married shortly after, and she'd moved to Argentina. Their story was super romantic.

"See you Monday at half past six. *Now* you can go back to speaking Spanish."

"Castellano," a boy called from the back.

I cringed, but Mrs. Prescott laughed and said, "Yes, Castellano. Once my brain learns something, it's hard to switch."

Around me the class laughed. We all knew how true that was.

The sounds of chatting filled the air while I gathered my stash of flash cards and the pile of books I'd brought from school. Seventh grade was in the late shift that got out at five thirty, which meant that by the end of English, I was already exhausted and ready for a break.

Halfway to the door, Nahuel caught up to me and said quietly, "Good night, María Emilia."

He kept walking, but I saw a pinkish hue spread across the brown skin of his face. My cheeks went pomegranate mode.

"Good night," I replied a second too late.

Nahuel passed Violeta, who was waiting for me in the doorway. She had the *most* expressive face in the world. Dozens of embarrassing questions were painted on it. I hoped Nahuel couldn't read any of them.

Violeta clutched my arm as we walked out to the lobby and exclaimed, "What was that all about?"

I playfully shoved her. "Violeta! Quiet!" A flutter of tiny wings tickled my tummy, making me giggle.

Mrs. Prescott, who had followed us out, looked as if she were trying not to laugh.

"Nahuel said good night to you!" Violeta squealed.

"Stop it!" I said, watching Mrs. Prescott and Alejandra, the receptionist, exchange an amused look. "He was just being nice."

Violeta wiggled her eyebrows like a dork. "I'll say. Ah, María Emilia! Your life is practically perfect!"

"Of course it is! I have you, don't I?" I hugged her with one arm, looking out the window to see if Lela was on her way.

Violeta was a week younger than me. We had photos of our moms, who were cousins too, with smiles as big as their bellies, and then of us two together, from the cradle we'd shared during naptimes at Lela's house to our last year of elementary school. Two peas in a pod. Even if I occasionally wished she came with a mute button, I couldn't imagine my life without her.

Violeta's dark eyes sparkled when she looked at me. "You're the luckiest girl in the world! You're beautiful. You have the two sweetest little brothers, perfect grades, and such a perfect voice you got the choir solo at graduation. The cutest boy ever said hello to you . . ." She ticked off all these blessings on her fingers. She didn't sound jealous at all, and my heart quivered. To me, she was the prettier and smarter of us.

She didn't see it though. She was so hard on herself.

"Knock on wood," I said, rapping my knuckles against her head, part superstition, part joke. What if because she mentioned my life was perfect, everything fell apart? "Your life is perfect too."

Before Violeta could contradict me, Mrs. Prescott sneezed. Violeta's eyes went wide with surprise, as if she had just noticed our super-proper teacher could hear our conversation all along.

"Sorry," she mouthed at me.

I tried to suppress a smile.

After a few seconds of embarrassed silence, Mrs. Prescott looked up from her phone and asked in English, "Do you need to call your ride, girls?"

Although we weren't in the classroom anymore, I made an

effort to reply in the best accent I could muster. "No, thank you, Mrs. Prescott. My grandmother is on her way."

Lela was never late.

In that moment, Tía Yoana, Violeta's mom, opened the door and a gust of frigid August air blasted over me.

Tía Yoana and my mom looked a lot alike. Some people thought they were twin sisters. They both had the same pointy face, almond-shaped brown eyes, and high cheekbones. Short and slender, Tía kept her hair long and curly, while my mom kept hers in a chin-length bob of straight black hair. Violeta looked a lot like them, while I'd taken after my dad. I was taller and curvier than Violeta, but some people said we had the same laughter, explosive and loud.

"Mami!" Violeta said, surprised, and kissed her mom on the cheek.

I gave her a kiss too, and she smiled and said, "Hola, mi amor."

"Hola, Tía," I said, grabbing my backpack. "Bye, Mrs. Prescott."

Tía Yoana's eyes widened. "Actually, Mimilia, Lela is still coming to get you."

Instant disappointment. Why did she insist on calling me Mimilia, the pet name the family had given me when I was a baby? Violeta and I were both trying to go by our proper names for high school, and the time to get into the habit was now. Tía didn't get it though. Or she didn't want to get it, according to Violeta, whose nickname was Leti.

I wasn't fast enough to hide my feelings, but at least I didn't whine like Violeta, who said, "But why? We had it all planned out. Can't she come home for a little bit?"

Tía shook her head and grimaced. "I'm sorry, my loves. Mimilia's parents are coming home from Buenos Aires tonight."

My breath hitched. "They're coming home already? So everything went okay?"

Tía smiled like a cat and made a motion as if zipping her lips.

I didn't know how to react. I didn't even know what "okay" would mean to me. My parents had gone to the capital for an interview at the US embassy. Mami had been offered a position to teach Latin American history at a college in the United States. Although in the past the opportunity to live in another country had excited me, at the end of seventh grade—as my family got closer to actually doing it—the idea now terrified me. Depending on the visas, and on the meeting today, we might be moving our lives to an entirely new country. And we might not.

Violeta sent me a pained look. "Call me as soon as you know." She grabbed her backpack and coat. "I won't be able to sleep!"

"As soon as I know." I nodded.

Tía gave me one last kiss and took Violeta's hand. "See you later, Mimilia. I'm sure we'll talk."

When they left, I gazed out the window, trying to make Lela materialize before Mrs. Prescott asked me about my parents. But it seemed Mrs. Prescott couldn't resist the mystery. She asked, "Were your parents in Buenos Aires to go to the embassy?"

How did she know about the embassy?

She must have read the question in my eyes because she said, "Your mom told me, of course. I helped certify the translation for a few of the forms."

That made sense. There had been dozens and dozens of

forms for each of the five of us. The visa requirements changed every month, it seemed. It was hard to keep up with the ever-moving target. Hard and expensive.

"Thanks," I said. Lela said that the Zonda wind makes people do and say unusual things. Maybe that's why I blurted out, "Getting the right seals for my birth certificate was a pain."

"You were born in Miami, right?"

The receptionist glanced at me with curiosity, and I hesitated. It wasn't a secret that I'd been born in the United States, but I never talked about it. It didn't really matter. I didn't even remember being there. I was from Mendoza like my family for generations before me.

But I couldn't ignore Mrs. Prescott's question.

"My parents were on vacation and I came early," I said, nodding. "I was in the NICU for a few weeks before we could all come back home."

Home. *This* was my home.

Home wasn't the same as the place where you were born.

Besides, like Violeta had said, my life was perfect. Here. Now.

The wind howled outside, making the naked trees bend

under its force. There was no sign of my young, energetic abuela, and I was getting a little worried.

"Are you excited to live in the United States?" Mrs. Prescott asked.

In the span of two seconds, the whole spectrum of my emotions surged in me. I crossed my arms. "When I was little, I dreamed about living in Miami or New York . . . and now . . ."

A black car pulled up to the curb and honked.

A smile lit up Mrs. Prescott's whole face. "Oh, I'm sorry. My ride is here, María Emilia. See you next week." She waved as she swept out the door. "And make sure you practice lots and lots of conversation. Your accent is getting so much better."

The song of victory I thought had died down reawakened in me. We'd been speaking English the whole time, and I hadn't even noticed. Usually when I spoke, I was so self-conscious about my accent I forgot the right words.

Just when I was about to ask the receptionist if I could use the office phone to call Lela, the door swung wide open, and a whirlwind entered—not the atmospheric kind. It was my two brothers, Mateo and Francisco. The sound level at the institute went from spa peaceful to fútbol-stadium decibels, but Alejandra smiled at the sight of them. At six and seven, they were pure unbridled enthusiasm. I'd been an only child for a long time, and now I treasured my little brothers—even when they were annoying.

"Mimilia," they exclaimed in unison when they saw me. "You're never going to guess the news!"

CHAPTER 2

My brothers' voices rose and rose in volume and pitch as they struggled to speak over each other. My ears rang.

Pulling my best trick, I put my hand up and my brothers went silent. Papi called me the brother whisperer for good reason.

"Tell me outside," I said, waving goodbye to Alejandra.

Lela sent me a grateful smile and led us out of the lobby. As soon as we opened the door, the wind snapped my uniform skirt. I placed a hand firmly against it even though I was wearing shorts underneath. After last week's Zonda, the wind had turned cold and humid, bringing snow to the Andes and biting cold to the valley.

Lela and I sandwiched Mateo and Francisco between us, and holding hands, we made our way to the bus stop.

I had so many questions, but I didn't know what to ask first.

My brothers' chatter continued on the bus. "Mami's bringing us a big surprise from Buenos Aires. Maybe it's a Messi jersey," Francisco said.

Mateo shrugged. "I want a Cristiano Ronaldo one."

Francisco puffed up his cheeks, gathering strength for an argument about who the greatest fútbol player of all time was. The two of them went full steam until they had everyone on the bus laughing. One man in a suit and tie told them neither one was the GOAT. The best was Maradona.

To stop my brothers from arguing back, Lela gave them her phone. That was the only way to keep them quiet the rest of the ride.

With them entertained, she snuggled me close to her with one arm. Her coat smelled of lemon-lavender fabric softener. "Now tell me about the test," she said.

I broke into a smile and showed her my perfect score.

"Your skills in English are going to come in handy," she said softly, arching an eyebrow.

"You mean . . . ? Is that the surprise Mami is bringing from Buenos Aires?"

"All I can say is that your mami sounded happy when we spoke on the phone."

"What did she say exactly, Lela?" I asked.

My parents' news would change our lives, one way or another. Teaching in the United States was one of Mami's biggest dreams. But Lela wouldn't be coming with us. There would be heartbreak with either possibility, yes or no, and I didn't know how to prepare myself for both at once.

"She and your papi will tell you in person soon, mi amor. Be patient."

As the oldest sibling, I was used to having to set an example for my brothers, but now I wished I could throw a mini tantrum so Lela would tell me.

"How soon? When will they get here?"

"It's a long ride from Buenos Aires," Lela said, patting my arm. "They'll be home tonight."

I sighed and looked out the bus window. Even in the distance, the Andes looked majestic in their mantle of new snow. Papi had climbed Aconcagua when he was in college. He'd promised me that in October, before the weather turned too hot, we'd hike to the first Aconcagua base camp. I'd been wanting to do it for a long time. After Lela's news, I worried I wouldn't have the chance.

My heart felt heavy in my chest. The happiness of getting a perfect score felt like a memory from last year. Nahuel's wink now didn't even make me smile.

The song I'd started writing still hummed quietly in the back of my mind, but I couldn't come up with any words to add. So I let the melody ring. Some feelings are too hard to put into words. Music is a language in itself.

Soon, it was our stop. Pretending they were birds in the blowing wind, the boys flapped their arms as they ran to the front door of the house Lela shared with us, where Mami had grown up.

"Hurry, Lela," Mateo said, jumping in place, his lips chattering.

Lela fumbled with the keys to the iron door and then the front door.

"Careful that Estrellita doesn't sneak out!" I warned as my hair whipped into my face.

Our cat Estrellita, Little Star, behaved more like a dog than a cat and always waited for us at the door. But when Lela finally opened the door, Estrellita wasn't there to greet us.

"She must not have heard us," Lela said.

Estrellita's absence felt like a missing tooth. The last thing I needed was for her to get lost in a storm.

"Estrellita!" I called.

Although I tried to keep my voice calm, my brothers must have sensed my rising panic. They started running all over the house calling out for her. They wanted to help, but their yelling would only keep her away. In her old age, Estrellita had become extra sensitive to loud sounds.

"Check this out!" Francisco exclaimed, and pulled me by the hand toward the laundry room.

He pointed at the window, which was open just wide enough to let in the wind—and let out a small cat. A layer of dust coated every surface, and I noticed a set of paw prints along the floor leading to the window.

"She's gone . . ." Mateo said, and then he shrugged. "But she always comes back. You know she does."

My brothers left me alone in the laundry room and headed

to the kitchen to get their merienda, the afternoon snack. I stood by the window for a second, looking out.

Estrellita had been my friend ever since I'd found her stuck in the tree that still spread its branches over the yard. She was playful like a kitten even though Papi thought she was about six or seven years old by then.

The day before, my best friend from kindergarten, Ludmila, had moved to Spain. I was devastated. No one had told me she was leaving until we went to the airport to say goodbye to her family. I never saw or heard about her again. That night I cried myself to sleep, and Lela had suggested I wish upon the Southern Cross constellation for another good friend. And *bam*, there was my cat, who followed me around like a shadow, my constant friend and companion, always getting into some kind of adventure.

I placed my hand on the window, debating whether or not to close it in case Estrellita returned. I ended up closing it. She always went around to the front door anyway, but not until she was ready to come home.

"Lela?" I said, coming back to the kitchen, where my brothers were already eating toast and watching cartoons.

"Yes, mi amor?" Lela was getting the mate ready.

Mate—that would be MAH-teh—is an herbal tea and a staple in our house, like in many places in South America. She filled the mate gourd with herbs and a pinch of sugar, and placed the filtered straw inside it. The water heated up in the red electric kettle on the counter.

"Estrellita's not in the house and the laundry window was open."

Lela clicked her tongue. "She snuck out again."

"Why does she keep going out? It might snow . . ."

Maybe she heard in my voice how close I was to crying because she turned around, gathered me in her arms, and kissed the top of my head. "Ay, chiquita . . . Estrellita hasn't been feeling well . . . Sometimes when a cat leaves the house, it's because they're ready to go to heaven."

"No, Lela! Don't say that!"

But deep in my heart, I wondered if I hadn't knocked my knuckles hard enough against wood. Like Violeta had said, my life was perfect. Until something shifted. I felt change coming my way like the dreadful heaviness before a storm, when nature seems to hold its breath. And when it blew again, how far would it carry me? I hoped my roots were deep enough to keep me grounded.

After a merienda of hot chocolate and toast, I helped my brothers with their homework. Their little lives were so simple. One plus one. Connect the dots. Draw a picture of your family. To them, everything was exciting.

Mine seemed so complicated. I was equal parts worried about my cat, excited for my parents to come back with their news, and dreading their arrival.

The evening turned into night. Dinner came and went, but there was no sign of my cat—or my parents. My brothers were already in bed when my phone chirped, and I jumped with surprise.

"Who is it?" Lela asked, sounding as anxious as I felt.

I checked the screen. "Only Violeta."

News yet?

Nothing.

I'm going to bed, but I'll have my phone. Let me know as soon as your parents are home.

Violeta and I had no secrets. We hadn't talked a lot about

our potential move, but she knew everything I knew.

I headed outside to check for Estrellita again. It hardly ever snowed in the valley, but now drops of snowy rain prickled my skin. I tried not to think of the dark highway, slick from the weather, but I couldn't help it. I wished for my Estrellita to be back so she could snuggle with me. But the only sounds were the raindrops on the carport tin roof and the creaking tree limbs dancing in the storm.

I went back inside and got in bed, but sleep escaped me.

Lela sat next to me on the bed that had once been my mom's. She brushed her hand over my head and sang "Ninna Nanna," an old, old lullaby her grandma had brought from Italy as a young girl, except that now Lela sang the lyrics in Spanish.

I joined her softly.

When the last note's echo died down, she said, "You have the voice of an angel, María Emilia."

"I got it from you, Lela."

She kissed my forehead. My chest glowed with so much love for her, and I closed my eyes to savor the moment. Finally, I was able to doze off.

The sound of the key turning in the front door awoke me with a jolt.

I couldn't see the wall clock in the darkness, so I followed the soft murmur of voices to the kitchen.

When I locked eyes with Mami, her face broke into the biggest smile.

"It was a yes!" she said. "We got the green light to move to the United States!"

From behind her, I saw Papi's tired eyes. In his arms, he held a sleepy Estrellita.

CHAPTER 3

While I prepared the mate, Mami and Lela chatted excitedly in the kitchen. The sweet scent of herbs—yerba, spearmint, and burrito—tickled my nose. Next to me, Papi made sandwiches with leftover milanesas from dinner and handed one to Mami. Estrellita finished eating the cheese I'd left in her bowl and curled up to rest right where she was.

I wished I could sleep too, but my mom's news had rattled me. Thoughts of change fluttered in my head like a swarm of chatty finches.

"Let's put Estrellita *and you* in bed," Papi said, always observant.

"I'm not tir—" I started saying, when a yawn interrupted me.

Papi smiled and carefully carried Estrellita to the laundry

room to place her in the basket that once upon a time had been my brothers' bassinet. She pried her eyes open, fighting sleep, and when she saw me next to her, she blinked. My heart bloomed with an overwhelming love for my cat.

Blinking is how cats say *I love you*.

Papi brushed her head, and Estrellita curled up like a crescent under his touch. She was tan all over, except for her face and ears and paws, which deepened into rich brown points. We'd always suspected she had some Siamese cat genes in her.

"She was waiting outside, but I think you couldn't hear her because of the wind," Papi said.

"Why would she run out?" What was there out in the world that called to her when she was so loved in our family?

"Sometimes when they're old, they do strange things," Papi said. "Like running out in the night even though a storm is coming."

"Lela said that too."

"Estrellita thinks she's a puma," he said.

I smiled at the image of my old cat prowling around the neighborhood, thinking she was a fierce big cat.

Papi draped his arm over my shoulder and pulled me close. I nuzzled against him. The familiar scent of his leather jacket still held the chill of the storm outside. He'd grown up in an estancia in San Lorenzo, close to Rosario, almost twelve hours away from Mendoza. He knew about animals, and even though he wasn't a vet, the neighbors always came over with questions when their pets were sick or hurt.

Papi had met Mami at the University of Rosario. When they graduated, they'd moved to Mendoza, where Mami's family was established for generations and generations. He'd learned to love the sierras and the mountains, and the dryness of the air.

All these years later, his voice still carried the soft sounds of las pampas in the way he pronounced the *y*'s and *ll*'s, and clipped the *s*'s out of the ends of his words.

"Are you ready to go to sleep?" he asked.

I shook my head. This was one of those life-changing moments, and I couldn't miss it.

"Come, then," he said, holding my hand.

Mami and Lela were waiting for us in the kitchen.

"We brought some facturas from Buenos Aires, mi amor,"

Mami said, and patted the seat beside her. "Look, tortitas negras from Manuelita."

My mouth watered at the sight of the sweet biscuits sprinkled with blackened sugar. Manuelita was my favorite bakery even though I'd never actually been there. Besides being an expert in animals, Papi liked to bake and cook, and was a chef by profession. But his tortitas just didn't turn out the same. He said it was the water. When either one of my parents went to Rosario or Buenos Aires, to visit family or to present at a conference, they brought tortitas negras back.

When I bit into one, sweetness flooded my senses and comforted me. Mami continued talking with Lela, telling her about the interview at the embassy.

"Our papers were in order, signed, and stamped."

"And triple-stamped," Papi said. "Especially Mimilia's birth certificate."

"What a nightmare!" Lela exclaimed, and shivered.

The odyssey of my birth certificate still gave us chills. Because I'd been born in the United States and I had an American passport, I needed an immigrant Argentine ID to register for high school. My new identification card looked identical to my family's and friends' cards except that in the citizenship space it said *American*, meaning, the United States. It also had *EXTRANJERA* in red block letters on the right-hand corner: Foreigner. Outsider.

To get that document, my birth certificate needed an official seal from the United States. One of my parents' friends who lived in Miami got it for me. But the certificate kept getting lost in the mail. Until one of Papi's colleagues came to hike Aconcagua last year and brought it in person.

"After reviewing the papers, the lady said to come back in a couple of hours." Mami passed el mate back to Lela, who poured more hot water in and passed it to Papi.

Papi chuckled. "I asked her for a clue of what the decision would be, so we could prepare ourselves for the disappointment, you know?"

I held my breath even though I knew the outcome.

"She winked at me, and said, 'Felicidades, Profesora,' in the most perfect Rosarinian accent." Mami patted Papi's arm. "And when we went back, all the passports had the visa."

"Except for Mimilia's, our little Yankee," Papi said, and I smacked his arm playfully.

They were all happy, but I had so many questions. Especially after Mami said, "With our flight only a week away, there's so much to do. The next few days will be a whirlwind—"

"Next week?" It felt like the chair had vanished from underneath me. One week?

Mami winced. "I need to report for class on September third, right after their Labor Day. There is so much to do, like sign you kids up for school and get all the paperwork ready. There's so many new forms waiting to be filled!"

Papi said softly, "We knew it would be soon, Mimilia, if everything worked out."

I had been so wrapped up in *yes or no* that I'd forgotten to focus on *when*. Of course it would be soon. But one week? I didn't say anything. Papi stroked my hair. "I'm sure you have so many questions, but you still have school tomorrow," he said. "It's time for bed now."

School! What was going to happen to my graduation now?

"But, Papi," I said. "This is the worst timing ever."

Mami was talking with Lela, but when she heard me and looked in my direction, her joy-filled eyes turned sad.

She had been waiting for this opportunity all her life.

The fight left me like a puff of wind.

"I'm sorry," I said. "Good night."

"Good night. Dream with the angels," the three of them said with a combination of sadness and love that made my eyes prickle.

Before I started crying, I quickly kissed them and went to bed.

Estrellita joined me immediately. I snuggled next to her, thoughts blaring in my mind.

How was I going to tell Violeta that I wasn't going to be around to help her pass her English exams? Ever since we were little, we planned for our trip to Córdoba at the end of seventh grade, a tradition before high school. I would just have to miss it?

How would I tell the rest of my class that I wasn't going to sing the solo? That I wasn't going to be at our graduation at all?

And the part I really hadn't let myself think about: I knew Lela wasn't planning to come with us.

How could I leave the best parts of my life behind?

It was true my ID said I was una extranjera, a foreigner. But this was my home.

The winds of change blew harder and harder, and I tried to hold on to my life as it was. But it already felt like it was slipping through my fingers.

CHAPTER 4

The next day on the ride to school, Violeta held my hand. Telling her that we'd be moving in one week had left me breathless.

Tía was on the phone with one of her clients as she drove with her Bluetooth headset on. I'd hoped she'd help me figure out my feelings like she helped so many as a therapist, but by the sound of it, the conversation wouldn't be over any time soon.

The pressure in my chest that had started yesterday was heavier today. I couldn't breathe deep enough.

"Are you okay?" Violeta said when she finally looked in my direction and saw me rubbing my chest.

I inhaled but the knot lodged there wouldn't budge. I sent her a weak smile.

All morning over text Violeta had insisted I tell my parents I wasn't moving with them. But when she saw me, she must have understood that in this situation, I had no vote. And I needed her. "I don't understand why this had to happen right now. I'm sorry," she said. "I know how important graduation and the solo are to you."

"They are. It's just that there are other things that are more important. Like my mom finally having a job again." I was only repeating the words my mom had said to me this morning.

"Maybe you can stay with Lela," she said. "Or with us. Right, Mamá?"

Tía nodded, but then, as if she'd realized what she was doing, she shook her head, still on her call.

"I'm going to miss you so much!" Violeta said, her face turning a shade of the color she'd been named after.

By then, we'd arrived at school.

"Have a good afternoon, girls," Tía called from the car. And then looking at me added, "Mimilia, remember you're about to go on the greatest adventure of your life."

I knew she was right, and I was excited. But secretly, I was also scared. What kind of adventures had life prepared for me?

All afternoon, I sat in class looking attentive, but my mind raced as I thought of all the loose ends I needed to tie up before I left. Things were happening too fast. The whirlwind Mami had anticipated was knocking me around without control.

"Are you not feeling well, María Emilia?" Señorita Nancy, my social studies teacher, asked when the recess bell rang. "You're always humming while you work, and today I've missed your melodies. Is everything all right?"

What I needed was a remote control that could pause time. I needed to process what was happening to me. In the movies, the heroes jump at the chance of an adventure. But here I was, dreading the changes coming my way. But how to say that to Señorita Nancy? I made an effort to smile at her, but my chin quivered embarrassingly.

"Oh no. Don't cry," she said softly, kneeling next to my desk. All around us, the class was heading out to recess, and every girl's eye was on me. Violeta was nowhere to be seen. "Did anything happen at home?"

"María Emilia?" Mami's voice called from the classroom door. One way or another, Mami was always there when I needed her.

Violeta had said I could stay with Lela or Tía Yoana and her, but the truth was, I'd never survive apart from my brothers and parents.

My family was my life. And Estrellita was part of my family.

How could I leave her behind—but how could we take her—now that she was so old?

Mami walked in my direction, looking worried. I had to fix this. I cleared my throat and said, "Señorita Nancy, it's just that we're moving, and I'm sad about my cat, Estrellita. I don't want to leave her behind."

"And can't you bring her along?" the teacher asked my mom.

Mami frowned. "We were planning on it, but she's so frail, the long flight won't be the best for her. Papi already asked the vet," she said, looking at me.

I sobered up at the news. If my dad had asked the official vet, then there was no argument.

"Oh," I managed to say, while my mom explained to the teacher about our big move across the hemisphere.

"What an opportunity!" Señorita Nancy exclaimed. "Besides, in the United States, you can get another pet, right?"

Why did adults think the furry members of a family were less important than the human ones? For a long time, other than Violeta, Estrellita had been my only friend. Now that she was old and sick, would she think I was abandoning her? I couldn't stand the thought of her waiting for me at the window.

"I know this didn't come at a convenient time," Mami said to me in a soft voice.

"I understand, Mami," I said, taking her hand.

If it was so easy for my head to get it, why was my heart giving me such a hard time?

"I'm sorry, María Emilia," Mami continued. "I don't want to check you out early, but I have to stop by your brothers' school too. There's so much to do . . ."

Her face reflected the storm raging inside me. This situation couldn't have been easy on my parents either. They were trying their best for the whole family. How could I make things more complicated? They needed me. How could I be so selfish and ungrateful to complain about a life anyone might want?

I decided right then that I would not complain again.

I ran my fingers under my eyes.

"It's okay, Mami," I said. "At least we're together."

"That's the right attitude," Señorita Nancy said cheerfully.

After a polite goodbye to my teacher, I gathered my things and followed my mom out the door.

Mami held my hand, and we walked side by side in silence, each lost in our thoughts.

Finally, she cleared her throat and said, "Your principal was so sad that you won't get to sing in the graduation show. She asked if you'd like to sing at your goodbye party . . ."

It was hard enough to contain my emotions when I spoke, but when I sang, I let my whole heart soar like a bird stretching its wings. If I was going to do a good job singing, I couldn't rein in my emotions. There were many unknowns in the future, but one thing I knew for certain: I didn't want to cry in front of the whole school. I wanted my friends to remember me as bubbly, happy María Emilia and not the one who cried when life offered amazing opportunities.

"I don't know if that would be a good idea . . ." I said, and Mami didn't press me for more.

All the way to my brothers' school to collect their report cards, my mom and I listed the things we needed to do and assigned the best family member for the job.

The concrete to-do list helped me feel better.

The boys' teachers were equally sad that we were leaving, but unlike Señorita Nancy, they had a completely different version of what was really happening.

"Oh my goodness!" the principal exclaimed, laughing, the color returning to his pale face. "I thought . . . So all of you are . . . ?"

Mami's cheeks were flaming as she explained, "Yes, yes, we're all moving!"

Francisco and Mateo looked at each other and shrugged.

"Mimilia's not staying back, then?" Francisco asked.

They both looked at me with such sadness and concern that I didn't even have the heart to joke. "No, mi amor," I said. "I'm not staying behind. Do you think I'd miss this adventure?" They hugged me before the words were completely out of my mouth.

The four of us walked home, my brothers saying goodbye to every park, playground, and treat shop we passed. In spite of the cold spell that had fallen over the city, soon the trees would bloom. I wouldn't be here to see the city change from winter into spring and summer, my favorite seasons.

I wouldn't hike to the first Aconcagua base with my dad.

I'd never sing in the concert or graduate with my friends.

Nahuel and I wouldn't even have the chance to become friends now.

So many things I wouldn't get to do. Things I'd looked forward to for so long.

When we arrived home, Estrellita was sleeping next to the space heater.

She looked so frail and tired. Mami had been right. I hadn't needed the vet to confirm it, but I didn't want to see the truth. My cat would never make the long flight. It would be selfish of me to pluck her out of the comfortable life she had.

At least she and Lela would keep each other company while we were gone.

"Tía Yoana and Violeta will be here soon to help us pack, but let's get a head start," Mami said.

"Pack clothes for how long?" Francisco asked. "Mama, how long will we be gone?"

Mami bit her lip. "My contract is for one year."

"I don't have three hundred and sixty-five underwears!" Mateo exclaimed, his big brown eyes looking bigger than usual.

Mami laughed at my brother's words and said, "Just pack underwear and socks for a couple weeks. We'll do laundry and get new stuff too, you know?"

"New stuff!" Francisco jumped in the air.

"Yes!" Mateo exclaimed, and took off running frantically around the house, trying to fit all his stuffed animals, LEGO, action figures, *and* the leather football the Three Kings had brought last year inside a tiny toy suitcase.

"Only a year, Mami?" I asked.

Mami ruffled my hair as she took out a giant photo album from her backpack and put it back on the bookshelf. "Initially," she said. "For now, yes. I'm hoping to get a permanent position though—"

The doorbell rang and Mami went to answer it. It was Tía Yoana and Violeta.

When the three of them came back to the kitchen, Mami gazed at my brother's suitcase and in a firm voice said, "Remember they have soccer balls where we're going. You need to pack clothes. Winter clothes, children. *The essentials*," she added, looking at me.

Everyone's definition of *essential* was different. My mom

and Tía Yoana laughed when they went over the things my brothers had crammed in their backpack pockets, but emotion swelled inside me. Who could judge that little notes from frenemies at school and fútbol teammates weren't important? The scraps of paper and cheap toys contained their little hearts, and I hurt for them.

Violeta following me closely, I went back to my room and took out my old journals from my suitcase and put them in a box in my closet.

"I'll make sure everything stays just as you left it," Violeta promised me, and gave me a big hug. "I'll miss you, but I'm excited for you."

We stood in silence in front of my closet. I didn't know how to start. And then she gave me a package I hadn't noticed she was holding. "Here. So you can think of me."

I opened it and saw it was her favorite shirt. A button-down with hummingbirds and butterflies printed in pastel colors. As if I needed something to remember her when she'd forever be in my heart.

"Thank you," I said, and placed it first in my suitcase.

* * *

The news of our move spread to family and friends, and during the next few days, our house was buzzing with the sounds of chatter, music, and laughter as everyone helped us pack and clean the house.

The night before the flight to Buenos Aires, our first stop, five big suitcases sat by the front door. Tío Gonzalo, one of Papi's friends, would put them in his pickup truck to take to the airport when the time came.

With nothing else to do, I finally locked myself in my room to say goodbye to my life as I knew it.

For the last week, and after her last escapade the night of the storm, Estrellita had mostly slept around the clock.

I was an optimist, but something in the back of my mind told me she had already said goodbye to the things she had loved when she was young and was ready to cross the rainbow bridge soon. Not even the cheese I had brought her for a late-night snack was enough to wake her up. She seemed so tired. She'd had a long life as a cat. But I wasn't ready to say goodbye.

The familiar lullaby left my lips with modified lyrics for my precious cat. "Ninna nanna, ninna, oh, esta gata, a quién se la doy?"

My breath shuddered. In spite of the lyrics, I never wanted to give my cat away to anyone. Estrellita blinked at the sound of my voice and started purring when I petted her soft fur. Once again, I wished with all my heart for a way to stop time.

Not forever.

I wouldn't be happy forever frozen in this sad night, the saddest night of my life. But I wanted to pause it long enough to take a deep breath and have my chance to say goodbye to this part of my childhood that was ending.

A soft knock on the door startled me. A second before I burst into tears. But duty called, and I swallowed all these feelings rumbling inside me. I'd have to wait for another moment to process it all. I couldn't let my parents think I was sad, that they were ruining my life.

"Come in," I said.

Lela's head poked through the cracked door. Her eyes were misty too. Since the moment we'd met at the airport when I was a baby, she and I had never been apart for more than a day. I already missed her smile every morning and the mushiest hugs in the world.

"Can I come in for a second?" she asked with a tentative smile.

I patted the bed next to me, and she sat. Everything had been such chaos; we hadn't really talked about how we were leaving her. She held a big white binder in her hands. Through the plastic cover, I saw the photo of a young girl from long, long ago. Even though she smiled, I recognized the sadness in her eyes. She and I looked nothing alike. Even in black and white her skin looked porcelain fair, and her eyes were light. My skin was the color of cinnamon, and my eyes were so dark they looked black. But somehow, looking at her was like seeing myself in a photograph.

"I brought you a little something," Lela said, and handed me the binder.

"What is it?" I asked, opening it and going through what looked like letters inside plastic page protectors.

Lela swallowed, like she needed a second to compose herself. I pressed my lips hard so I wouldn't cry. There was so much I wanted to tell her. There was so much I wanted to hear from her. I always thought we had all the time in the world, and now time ticked away.

A song lyric rang in my years. *Nothing good lasts forever* . . .

"Remember Nonna Celestina?" she asked.

The name took me back in a kaleidoscope swoosh of memories all the way to when I was even younger than my brothers. Back to when I still didn't have words to label my feelings. All I had kept from those years were scents and sounds. The name Celestina brought back the memory of lemons and a warm voice that echoed off the kitchen walls like the pitter-patter of raindrops on the patio tiles during a hot summer evening.

It took me a second to conjure her face, but I remembered her.

"Nonna Celestina was your mom! Mami's grandma," I said. "We had the same birthday!"

"You remember!" Lela said.

The October I turned five, Nonna Celestina turned one hundred years old. The local news station, Channel 7, had come to the house to interview her, and she'd been funny and snappy as always.

A few months later, she gently passed away in her sleep. After that, my family moved in with Lela, who'd said the house was too big now that Nonna was gone.

She was Lela's mom, and they had been the best of friends.

Lela always got teary-eyed when she talked about her, and now wasn't an exception.

"You still miss her so much," I said, patting Lela's hand. "I just remember her laughter and the songs she used to sing all the time."

"When you were little, she used to call you little Celestina. She remembered what it was like to be a small girl, even if it had been so long ago. This is the only photo we have of her when she was twelve."

"Like me!" I exclaimed, studying the photo.

How I wished I'd known my great-grandma better or that I could see a video of her at my age. My brothers and I had thousands of pictures of us taken every year. Papi had to keep buying external storage for the computer to hold all of them, all these memories of our lives. But she'd lived in different times.

Lela's mind seemed to be going in the same direction because she pointed at the binder and said, "We don't have a way to hear her voice when she was a child, but she wrote letters, which is almost the same thing. Nonna had lots to say. She wrote constantly to the people she loved who stayed behind in Naples when she moved to Argentina. She wrote to her own grandmother Nonna Rosa."

"Your mom's grandma would be my great-great . . ." I counted with my fingers, my mind already boggled by the pressing of time and distance.

Lela joined me in counting and then confirmed, "Great-great-great-grandma."

I couldn't picture it, so Lela grabbed a pen and a piece of paper from my nightstand and diagrammed it for me.

"Five people up the line from you," she said. "Nonna Rosa; then Mamma Anna-Maria; my mom, Celestina; me, Adelina; your mom, Pilar; and you, María Emilia. Nonna Rosa and Celestina were inseparable. They loved each other so much, they weren't going to allow an ocean, a lack of telephones, and unreliable mail carriers to keep them apart."

"How did they do it?" I asked.

"Letters," Lela said.

I turned page after page.

Lela continued. "I never read Italian. How sad I lost that connection to our culture, no? But my mom, who wasn't going to let a language barrier keep me from knowing her family, translated the letters for a school project I had to do long, long ago. We made copies for each little family branch. When your mom left for the university in Rosario, I made her a copy. Soon, your cousins wanted their own. I saved a copy for you. Your mom said you wanted to go back to the United States for college. Is that right?"

"When I said I wanted to leave, I didn't know what that really meant, Lela."

She tapped my chin, and I looked up at her. "Of course we never know what change feels like, Mimilia," she said. "Although I knew this day would come, I thought we had more time."

"Me too, Lela."

"But I think this is the perfect time for you to get to know my mom, your nonna Celestina. I thought what better than through her letters? She was twelve when she left Italy, and this photo was taken a few months after she and her family arrived in Rosario."

"Where Papi was born!"

Lela pointed at me on a family chart and then made a line all the way to Nonna Celestina. I read the small labels about great-great-grandparents that had room for sixteen people.

The number made me dizzy. It was impossible to imagine all those people who'd come before me, and whose names I didn't even know.

Lela kissed my forehead. "Put this in your backpack. I'm sure her words will help."

"Thank you, Lela. I'm going to miss you. I'm going to miss our charlas," I said, hugging her tightly and trying to memorize the warmth of her arms wrapped around me, the scent of her apple shampoo, and the way her voice lit up a whole room.

"We'll talk on the phone every day."

"It's not the same as talking face-to-face," I said.

Even Estrellita peeked at me when she heard the whining twang in my voice.

Lela laughed. "It's not the same, but it's better than nothing. It's not like when your mom left and all we had were calling cards or letters. You don't know the agony of processing photos only to realize none turned out, or that when they did, they got lost in the mail. Now we can video-chat whenever we want. I'll still see you *every day*."

A phone conversation would never compare to one of her

hugs or being together in the warmth of her kitchen. Still, I didn't want this last conversation to be sad.

Lela tipped my chin with her index finger once again. "I know this move is happening at a complicated time in your life. But I promise you that if you open your heart, a lot of opportunities will come for your family. Your mami got her dream job. Your brothers and you will get to perfect your English. And the five of you will be tighter than ever as you try to overcome the trials sent your way."

At the thought of trials, the little hairs stood on my arms and I shivered. Leaving Estrellita and Lela—leaving my life—was already the worst thing I could imagine.

Lela must have sensed my fears. "I know you will be the best example for your little brothers," she said. "Celestina's letters will help you. She went through the same thing, and in her words, you might find some light in this situation."

I hugged her again, inhaling her scent. "Thank you, Lela," I said. "I promise I'll see the bright side."

Lela left, and the house was quiet. I looked out the window, petting Estrellita beside me. It was so late and dark not even the stray dogs ventured outside. The cold, cold night sky sparkled. As if agreeing with all of Lela's words, the stars winked in and out.

Out of the darkness, a light streaked across the sky. I closed my eyes and tried to make a wish, but my heart was so full of feelings I didn't know what to wish for.

So I said aloud, "I'll save my wish for when I need it," to whoever was listening for wishes and made sure they came true.

I knew it was silly, but I felt just a little more prepared with a wish in my pocket.

CHAPTER 5

The whole neighborhood came out to say goodbye. My little brothers were so excited at being the center of attention without having to act out that they didn't know how to behave. Proof of that was their silence.

Like them, I was stunned to see tears on our friends' faces, and even people who I didn't know loved our family so much, like Don Basilio, the vegetable grocer from the stand two streets over, who had seen my mom and then me and my brothers grow up. But everyone was also happy that we were starting such a big adventure. Leaving Mendoza was a sad and a happy thing at the same time.

I promised myself not to cry because I was afraid that if I let one tear drop, the others would follow like an unstoppable waterfall.

I wished I'd made this promise after saying goodbye to dear Estrellita.

When I gave her the last snuggle, she gave me a head bump in return. She blinked a few times and then went back to sleep. My heart shattered in a million pieces. I swallowed the pieces before they turned into tears, and they knotted in my stomach.

Mami and I rode with Violeta and Tía Yoana to the airport. The whole ride Mami and Tía talked nonstop, as if they had to fit everything in.

In the back seat, Violeta and I held hands, knowing that words wouldn't be enough.

At the airport, where we took picture after picture, even more people turned out for goodbyes. Nahuel and the rest of my English class, including Mrs. Prescott, stood by the escalator. How I wished I'd asked her advice on how to leave everything behind and start from scratch. It was too late for that now.

I hugged all my friends, even Nahuel, with a blush.

I caught Violeta's eye as our flight was being called.

I don't remember who made the first move, but soon we were in each other's arms.

She hugged me tightly and whispered in my ear, "Don't forget me. I put a baggie with burrito in your backpack so when you drink mate you remember us."

As if I could ever forget her! My cousin and friend. I looked her in the eye so I could memorize her face, even though I hoped to still see her on my phone and the computer every day.

Finally, after Lela, Tía, and Mami hugged for the longest time, Lela squeezed me one more time.

"Let's go," Papi called, and held out his hand to me. I hitched my backpack on my shoulder. No matter how I folded my favorite clothes and how I arranged my books and old figurines in my one suitcase, I'd had to leave a lot of things behind. Still, my backpack was so heavy I concentrated on not tottering backward like my little brothers.

There was no more time, so I followed my family up the escalator. At the top, I looked back.

I wanted to memorize my last look of Lela, Violeta, Tía Yoana, the kids from school, and our neighbors and friends. Part of my heart was staying behind with them, and leaving it hurt like it was being torn apart. I waved and turned away.

I caught up with my family. An airline attendant was checking the passports.

"Ah," she exclaimed when she saw mine. "A little Yankee going back home?"

My cheeks warmed up. I was *leaving* my home. But it was also true I was going back to where I'd been born. Would the United States ever feel like my home?

"Everything's in order," she said, waving us forward. "Have a safe flight to Buenos Aires."

"You too," Mateo said, and in spite of the jumbled emotions, we all laughed.

Lela's advice of remembering the light rang in my ears. My own promise not to cry was enough for my eyes to stay dry.

But all my best intentions came crashing down as we stepped onto the first airplane.

"How are we sitting?" I asked, standing in the middle of the aisle, trying to figure out the configuration. Each side of the plane had two seats. Who was I going to sit next to?

I'd flown before, but I'd been a baby.

"Mami," I insisted. "Why am I the one left out?"

Mami looked over her shoulder as she tried to keep Francisco contained and said, "We can't have the boys sitting by themselves, mi amor." The look in her eyes begged me to understand, and although I didn't want to give in, I had no other choice.

My only consolation was that my seat was next to the window. I wanted to see Mendoza for the last time so I could remember it perfectly. Papi said there were beautiful mountains in Utah, where we were going, but I couldn't imagine anything as majestic as Los Andes.

Finally, the flight attendant said the cabin door was closed, and my heart leaped inside my chest. The plane engines roared, and I heard Francisco exclaim, "We're moving, Mami!" He giggled. He always laughed when he was nervous.

I crossed my arms tightly, wishing I could hold someone's hand for the takeoff. From across the aisle, Papi sent me a reassuring smile, but he had to go back to making sure Mateo didn't kneel on his seat as he looked out the window.

Finally, the airplane rose in the air, and after a few seconds, my ears popped. I unwrapped the piece of gum Mami had given me to chew so my ears wouldn't hurt. The strong mint made my tongue tingle.

Outside the small window, the sky was bright blue. Cotton-white clouds fell underneath the airplane as we climbed higher and higher, until the mountains looked like ant tracks on my brothers' nature table. I felt like a ribbon stretched and stretched from my heart to Lela, Estrellita, Violeta, and all those I loved and had left behind. And to the place that had been my home for twelve years.

Papi explained to Mateo how airplanes worked, and the explanation helped me not to panic when I thought about how high in the air we were. Francisco must have been asleep because Mami looked back over the seat in front of me and winked, tiredly. "I'm going to take advantage and nap."

What was it about parents and naps? How could she miss the spectacle out the window? How could she ignore the anxiousness of not knowing what was waiting for us at the end of our trip?

These questions and more thundered louder than the rumbling engines. To calm my nerves, I started humming "Ninna Nanna," and soon the song turned into the one

I'd started writing that day when I got a ten in English and thought my life was perfect. The lyrics came out in a tumble, inspired by the beauty of the sky and the swirling feelings inside me.

> *The mountain is hard to climb*
> *When you think you're all alone.*
> *In the darkness, the wind blowing,*
> *The doubts are louder,*
> *The fear is stronger.*

Just then, a rainbow wheel, a glory, appeared on my window. Mrs. Prescott had once told the class about them, but I never imagined anything so magical and beautiful.

I repeated the lyrics of my song over and over until the glory finally dissolved in a bank of clouds. But by then, my chest was warm and the knotted sadness in my stomach didn't bother me so much anymore.

Soon we were in Buenos Aires. The closest I'd ever been to the capital city was Rosario when we'd visited Papi's cousins. I'd wanted to catch a peek of the beautiful buildings and expansive parks, but our connection was tight. We had to run to our next gate, and we made it just in time. This airplane was way bigger than the first one. A lot bigger.

This time I was luckier and sat next to Papi and Mateo.

Mami and Francisco sat in a row toward the front of our section, next to a girl who had a companion dog. I never knew dogs could fly on airplanes, and my brothers were sad we hadn't brought Estrellita with us.

"She's too old for the trip," Papi explained again, but I could still hear a hint of sadness in his voice.

Mateo was jealous Francisco got to sit by a dog. He started crying in a mixture of overstimulation, emotional exhaustion, and sadness.

Finally, he fell asleep right after dinner, which he didn't even touch.

Papi put his headphones on and played a movie. Soon, he was asleep too.

And for my part, I grabbed the tiny strawberry ice-cream cup my brother had ignored and took out the binder of letters from Celestina. I brushed my fingers against the hand-writing in Italian and the translation my great-grandmother had typed on a typewriter. For the first time, I wondered why Lela hadn't learned her mother's own language.

Besides the language, what else from our heritage had been lost across the ocean and the passing of time?

The lights flicked off, and I turned on the feeble light above my seat to read the first letter.

Querida Nonna Rosa,

Mamma says we won't be able to post this letter until we arrive in Rosario, but I don't want to forget one detail. Already, the day we left seems a thousand years ago, and I hardly remember the smell of the ocean when we arrived at the port. After so long in this cabin, my nose is immune to the scents of so many cramped in a tiny space. I only notice how bad I stink when Babbo and I go up to walk around the main deck. The other day he pointed at Polaris and said that soon I wouldn't get to see it anymore. Every night after that, I wished on that star that this trip would be worth it. That my family might find somewhere to live and love in peace. Tonight, I couldn't see it anymore, but I know it's still there.

Mamma won't let the boys go up on deck because she's afraid they'll fall overboard. But considering they can't run around, Giovanni and Andrea have been angels. At night we sing to pass the time, and I've met a few other girls. Lina is from Trento, and sometimes it's hard to understand each other. If I don't understand the people from my own country, how am I ever going to understand the people in our new home?

Spanish sounds a little similar to Neapolitan, but when a girl from Andalucía was talking with her mother, I couldn't understand a single word of what they said. It's the same with the family from Lebanon whose daughter is about my age. I know her name is Nafiza, but we only communicate through signs and facial expressions.

At least when we sing together, everyone's heart can understand the feelings in the music.

Other than singing and sharing stories in the evening, there's not a lot to do. Last night some women were talking about health checks at the port. Mamma has been sick a lot, and now I worry for her.

All night and day, I have been restless, but when I saw the ocean, my heart calmed down. I wish we were staying close to the port when we arrive in Argentina. But Babbo says we'll have to travel north from Buenos Aires to meet his cousins in Rosario. Mamma says we'll be far from the ocean, but that there's a river so wide it seems like a sweet water sea. I wonder if I will like it there. I'm not happy that we'll arrive in winter when at home, the lemon trees were blooming already.

I miss you already, Nonna. As soon as you get this letter, write to me.

With love,
Celestina

I read the letter a couple of times, trying to imagine traveling across the world without any entertainment, having to wait weeks and months for news from back home. This trip was long, but we'd be at our new home within hours. And at least my brothers were entertained with the mini TVs on the back of the seats.

But I could understand how Celestina felt about the language. I'd studied English for years, but would my efforts be enough?

The rest of the trip, I watched a movie and tried to not read the subtitles.

Like Papi, I fell asleep halfway through. I startled when he shook my arm softly to wake me. "We arrived in Miami, pajarita. One more flight and a short four-hour drive, and we'll be home. And then you can sing like a little bird to your heart's content."

He meant to sound cheerful, but I winced, dreading the rest of trip. After sitting for ten hours with only a couple of bathroom breaks, my body was sore. I couldn't imagine another long flight and then a drive.

"When I grow up, I'll invent a teleporter," Mateo said, although he'd slept the whole time and had sprawled across the three seats like he was sleeping on a feather bed.

"Sign me up as your first customer," an old man said from the seat behind us.

Papi and I laughed, and Mateo flashed a toothless smile at me, his eyes sparkling.

The excitement in my brother's eyes turned into awe when we saw the multitude of people standing in line to go through customs.

True, it wasn't like in Celestina's letters, with doctors inspecting the newly arrived travelers and immigrants—I'd read a couple more about her arrival in Argentina. But Francisco was sniffling like he always did when we went on a trip, and he looked like a little wet bird. I tried to imagine what I would've done if my brother didn't pass the health inspection and we had to go back to Argentina. Even though I hadn't wanted to leave my life behind, we'd traveled too far to turn back now.

My parents had worked so hard for this, and being the oldest in my family, I had to be a good example.

I was trying to be at my best when it was our turn for the immigrations officer to go through our papers. When he saw my American passport, he said something I didn't catch. He had reddish hair and a mustache that wiggled when he talked.

"What?" I asked, inching closer so I could hear him better.

He repeated his words, and I looked at my mom in a panic. Could it be that my ears weren't working anymore? I had no trouble understanding movies or the flight attendants on the airplane.

Mami laughed and said in Spanish, "He asked why you didn't go through the American citizen line."

My heart jumped in my mouth when I thought I'd done something wrong. My first moments in the United States, and I was already messing up.

But the officer laughed, and said slowly, "Welcome home."

This time I understood him.

"Thank you," I said, and with flaming cheeks followed my family across the line that meant we were finally in the United States.

The next leg of the trip was the most exhausting yet. Francisco's sniffles had progressed into a cold that made his ears hurt. Mami and Papi took turns sitting with him, walking along the airplane aisle, and when we finally landed in the Salt Lake City airport, Mateo clapped, echoing everyone's feelings of relief.

Francisco had fallen asleep just as we landed, and Papi held him. Mami and I lugged the backpacks and carry-ons until we found a trolley.

But our trials weren't over. Although most of our luggage arrived safe and sound, an hour went by and there was still no sign of my blue suitcase with its red ribbon. Papi declared, "I'll make the report so we can get going."

"Let's wait a little longer, Papi!" I begged.

"Mi amor," Mami said in an exhausted voice. "The shuttle can't wait for us any longer. It's still a long drive, and we'd like to arrive in the daytime."

My brothers sent me looks of sympathy, and when I sighed as loudly as I could and nodded, Mami said, "Thank you. I knew I could count on you."

With a heavy heart, I helped Papi fill out the paperwork.

I looked at the uncooperative luggage carousel with resentment. What would I do if my suitcase didn't arrive in time for me to start school next week?

I didn't want to add to our family's worries, so I zipped my lips. But the special shirt Violeta had given me was in there.

What would Celestina do in my place?

I didn't want to waste the wish I kept in my pocket for my luggage, but my mood darkened as the shuttle drove to our new home, Red Ledges City. I looked at the mountains on both sides of the highway and understood why my parents had said this place looked like Mendoza. The mountains looked familiar but different at the same time.

Francisco slept for most of the ride, and our parents chatted with the shuttle driver excitedly. I tried to keep up with their conversation, but my head started pounding.

Mateo grabbed my hand. His was sweaty, and I tried to understand what was going on in his little head. He ended up falling asleep and resting his head on my shoulder, and I closed my eyes for a second.

Papi's gasp woke me up. "Look at that!"

On both sides of the highway, the red rock formations seemed like the surface of Mars. The pictures I'd seen online hadn't done them justice. The shuttle exited the highway, and it slowed down in a neighborhood of quaint little cottages under enormous trees. The sunset made the mountains glow red.

The driver turned onto a wide street where a trio of kids along with a little tan dog walked toward us: two boys and a girl. She had the reddest hair I'd seen in my life and seemed to be hitting imaginary drums with the thin sticks she carried. One of the boys played air guitar, and the three of them burst into laughter. The boy in a black shirt waved at the driver, and we soon lost sight of them.

Finally, the driver announced, "Welcome home!" The van

stopped in front of a pink two-story house, surrounded by trees and bramble bushes gone wild.

"I feel some Sleeping Beauty vibes," Mami said, smiling.

"We're just missing the turrets and buttresses. We have the princess," Papi said, looking in my direction.

Before I could add anything, Francisco woke up, suddenly alert.

"My favorite color!" he yelled, and unbuckled his seat belt in a swift move. He got out of the van so fast I just saw a blur of movement.

"Dibs on the rooms!" Mateo yelled, following Francisco and looking over his shoulder at me.

I stuck my tongue out at him.

An older woman who reminded me of Lela was waiting at the door. Her face broke into a giant smile when she saw us.

Although her accent in Spanish was different from ours, I finally understood someone who wasn't my family.

"Welcome home, Pilar and family!" she said.

CHAPTER 6

Our new house looked more like that of the good witch in a forest than a royal castle. Up close, the unmistakable whiff of fresh paint tickled my nose. A white porch wrapped around the house and in one corner an ancient-looking swing moved with the breeze, like a dog wagging its tail with happiness to welcome its family home.

The house had been waiting for us. Maybe I was tired from the trip, but my heart swelled with emotion.

I could hear my brothers running all over the house, as if the energy they had contained through more than twenty-four hours of sitting on planes, waiting at airports, and sitting again in the van was fizz from a shaken soda can.

Instead of joining them, I sat on the swing and looked up toward the mountains. The weeping willow's branches danced above me, and the leaves made a sound like waves crashing against the shore. I remembered how much Celestina loved the sea. What had she thought of her new house when she finally arrived in Rosario? Had it all been worth traveling across the Atlantic in a cramped boat for two weeks?

Papi and Mami chatted with the woman, Mrs. Campbell, who was the college liaison for new faculty. They trailed her into the house, and I stayed out on the porch to check out the neighborhood.

From the corner of my eye, I saw the little tan dog I'd seen before, but this time without the kids. It had a squishy little face and the perkiest ears I'd ever seen. It darted toward the neighbor's backyard before I could call to it. The houses here had no fences—each green yard blended into the next. No iron bars over the windows and doors. I hoped the kids I'd seen lived nearby. Every house had at least two floors. I remembered that in English the floors of a building were called stories.

Why? Was it because each floor had its own tale to tell?

What would my story be in this house? What kind of history would I leave behind?

My stomach growled. Without a functioning phone—no data—I had no idea what time it was. But judging by the sounds of my belly, and in spite of how light the sky still was, I sensed it was close to seven p.m. Ten in Mendoza. Dinnertime.

I was sure I could adjust to the three-hour difference quickly, but traveling north had also meant a change of seasons. Here in Utah, the hot, dry air felt like January in Mendoza—summer vacation, not the start of the school year. Now I would have to go from closing in on finals to starting a year all over again. It would be ages before I got a vacation. But I couldn't wait to go to school and make friends!

I headed toward the kitchen in search of food. The clock on the far wall pointed at six fifty-five. I had been right!

Mrs. Campbell was telling my parents, "While you're on campus, I'll show Miguel and the kids around town. First thing, we'll get groceries, sign the kids up at school, and go see the neighborhood. What do you think?"

The boys, still revved up, yelled, "Yes!" and jumped in place.

I couldn't believe how wired my brothers were; I was beat! The hours of travel and the emotional roller coaster were taking a toll on me, and I stifled a yawn.

As always, Papi got caught unawares and yawned loudly right after me, and we all laughed.

"I'm sorry," he said. "Getting here has been an odyssey."

Mrs. Campbell looked at me, and her eyes softened. "I'm sorry about your luggage."

A pang in my chest at the thought of my lost suitcase made my eyes tear up.

"Oh," Mrs. Campbell said, brushing my head with soft fingers. Her fair skin was speckled with freckles, and her smudged eyeliner made her green eyes look mossy and tired. It must have been a long day for her too. She continued. "I know your luggage will turn up. It always does. There's food in the fridge, and like I said, tomorrow morning I'll be here to help your dad sign you up for school. Hopefully you'll meet my granddaughter, Tirzah. She was actually here waiting for you with her friends, but they had to head back home."

"I think we saw them on our way here," Mami said.

"Most likely," she said. "Now . . . the Wi-Fi should be set up; the info will be on the router. What else can I do for you?"

"You've done enough, Montserrat. Thank you," Mami said.

"Thank you for everything," Papi and I echoed.

Mami and Papi walked Mrs. Campbell to her car. I nabbed an apple from a basket on the counter and turned to really take in the house.

The whole interior looked like a mountain cabin, with exposed ceiling beams and log walls. Quaint white curtains hung on the bottom half of the windows. It wasn't new by any means, but it smelled of fresh paint and sawdust. By the paint splatters around the baseboards, it seemed like it had been recently renovated.

My brothers had found a brand-new soccer ball and were kicking it back and forth in the kitchen. Mrs. Campbell, Montserrat like my mom had called her, must have left it for them. How nice of her!

"Careful, boys. You don't want to break anything," I warned.

"Mimilia, stop worrying!" Francisco exclaimed. "Why don't you go see the rest of the house? There's three bathrooms!"

"Three bathrooms?"

"Go see for yourself," Mateo challenged me.

I suspected they wanted to get rid of me so I wouldn't nag

them about playing inside the house, but I was curious and left them to explore.

Much of the ground floor was taken up by a big, open living room, with a soaring ceiling of wooden beams like I'd never seen before.

Down the hallway, the first bedroom I came across was also the biggest, which I assumed would be my parents'. Attached right to the bedroom was a large bathroom with two sinks and a bathtub.

En suite flashed into my mind.

Who knew all these strange words were waiting to jump to the spotlight as soon as I needed them?

We didn't have a bathtub at Lela's house, and I already imagined myself soaking in a bubble bath every night.

Excited, I ran out to see the room we'd be sharing. But when I found the second-biggest bedroom only featured two twin beds, I wondered where I'd sleep. I hadn't really thought about it before, but now I couldn't wait to find out.

I ran to the end of the hallway, and there was one of the other bathrooms Francisco had told me about. It only had a toilet and sink and was right next to a door that led outside, to a driveway. Maybe one day soon we'd have a car.

Mateo came up to me and took my hand. "Your room is upstairs, Mimilia. Come on, I'll show you."

I took his little hand and followed him up a set of wooden stairs. The dark glass on the windows gave the light a yellowish tint in which I saw dust dancing in spirals like fairy dust.

Finally, we arrived in an enormous space—*an attic*—with three big windows on one wall that framed the mountains, majestic and red with the glow of the setting sun. On the opposite wall was a round window and the willow tree waving hello.

A bed sat in a corner with a pretty pink-and-yellow duvet, and a small nightstand with a lamp in the shape of an elephant. A lamb's wool rug lay next to the bed. The wooden floors gleamed, and I detected the orange scent of wood polish.

"You have your own bathroom," Mateo said.

The sound of rapid footsteps preceded Francisco. "You're the luckiest!" he exclaimed, and plopped on my bed.

I started singing with joy, *"I'm the luckiest, yes, I know . . ."*

Until I saw his shoes left a black smudge on the duvet.

"Hey! Take your shoes off at least," I said, but he just grinned at me.

More footsteps announced Mami and Papi joining us in my room.

"Wow!" Papi said, his arms stretched out and turning in a big circle. "Look at you, pajarita! A perfect perch for my songbird."

I hugged him tightly. His blue polo shirt still smelled of Mendoza sunshine, and I inhaled deeply so I would never forget this scent.

He put his other arm around Mami, and my brothers, not wanting to be left out of the group hug, joined us too, quieted by our emotion.

My luggage was lost, but we had each other.

When the emotion was threatening to make me cry, Francisco's stomach growled. We all laughed.

"I'm hungry!" he said.

"In that case, let's go get a snack," Papi announced, and as the boys ran for the stairs, he said, "Although soon we'll have to adjust to the different mealtimes. People here eat at seven or so."

"Earlier!" Mami exclaimed. "I'm not joking," she added when we laughed again. My brothers and I looked at each other in disbelief.

"Until then, let's have some mate and a snack, and then showers for everyone!"

I lingered behind to peek into my bathroom. To my surprise, there was another bathtub. A bathtub just for me! The bathroom had a little window from where I could see the highway and traffic zooming by.

I had expected we'd live in an apartment, not a house so beautiful and cozy!

As I bounded happily to the bottom of the stairs, someone knocked on the front door.

CHAPTER 7

"Who can it be?" Mateo asked, alarmed.

"Maybe Mrs. Campbell forgot something," Francisco added, running to be the first one at the door.

"Wait," Papi said as Mami lengthened her step to get to the door before my eager brother. "Remember, Francisco, we still have the same rules as in Mendoza, you understand?"

Mami opened the door to reveal a large group of people on the porch. "Welcome!" they exclaimed in unison.

The rest of my family and I looked at each other smiling, and Mami replied, "Thank you!"

"Hello! We're the Bodens," said a slender woman about Mami's age, holding a tiny baby in her arms. She had light brown hair with highlights and an open, beautiful smile. Blond and blue-eyed, the man next to her was the tallest person I'd ever seen. A girl about my age looked just like her father but with darker hair, and a crowd of boys looked exactly like their mom, minus the long pink nails.

"We live right across the street," the woman continued. "There have been contractors working on the house for weeks, and today we saw the shuttle from the airport. We wanted to introduce ourselves."

At a sign from her, one of the boys, who must have been around ten, handed Mami a plate of cookies.

"How nice of you! Thank you! We're the Soler family," Mami said, and introduced each one of us. I gave a little wave when she said my name.

"Forgive us if it takes us a little while to learn your names. We don't speak Spanish, but I speak Russian and Stacy speaks Mandarin Chinese," Mr. Boden said.

Mrs. Boden blushed. "I don't really speak it anymore."

"She volunteers in the Chinese immersion program," he countered with a wink.

My family listened in silence, and I wondered if they too were listening as attentively as possible to catch every word.

Mrs. Boden—Stacy—went on to introduce their family.

The father was Scott, and the baby Lilly Ann. There were so many siblings that I couldn't catch all the boys' names. I understood what the dad had said about needing a little time to learn our names. I'd need time to learn theirs too.

Seven kids. Seven! Including the girl who seemed to be my age. When she smiled shyly, I saw colorful braces on her teeth.

"This is Ashley Jane, our eldest. She's going into seventh grade," Mr. Boden said.

My heart fell. It would've been nice to be in the same grade with a neighbor. "I'm going into high school," I said.

Mrs. Boden cocked her head to the side for a second and narrowed her eyes. "You look small for your age."

Not knowing what to say to that, I shrugged. I was average for my age back home, but compared to the neighbors I felt tiny.

"Anyway, nice to meet you, Ashley Shane," I said, and stepped toward the girl to kiss her on the cheek.

"Whoa, whoa," Ashley Jane said, putting her hand up. "Hello is enough. And it's Ashley Jane. With a *j*, not a *shh* sound."

My face went up in flames. "I'm sorry," I said. "I always have a hard time with the *j*." I still said it *shay*, and at the sound of my voice, my eyes prickled with embarrassment.

The lyric *Why you gotta be so mean?* rang in my mind.

I glanced at Mami, but she and Mrs. Boden were talking about the schools in the area. Apparently, the local elementary had a Spanish immersion program, in addition to Chinese.

Soon, everyone in my family had clicked with someone from the neighbors. Papi and Mr. Boden talked about the internet service. My brothers were talking with two Boden boys who looked identical, except one was a little taller than the other.

When I looked at Ashley Jane, racking my brain for something clever to say, she folded her arms.

I kept smiling even though I was so confused and, honestly, a little hurt. I hadn't meant to offend her. I was only being friendly.

To stop myself from crying in front of our new neighbors, I turned toward the conversation between Papi and Mr. Boden.

"The Jensens lived here for generations," Mr. Boden was saying. "We were a little surprised they agreed to rent the house outside the family circle. They were always a bit particular about the house. For years, they refused to get internet wiring. I know where they're coming from," he continued. "The house is a historical building after all."

All of a sudden, the house that had seemed so inviting and cozy turned into a fancy artifact. What would happen if my brothers broke a window playing fútbol inside the house, or I spilled something on the carpet?

"I'm glad they changed their minds!" Papi said with a relieved smile. "We love this house already, and we're all eager to stay in touch with our loved ones back home. That's not possible without the internet." I noticed that Papi's words were a little stiffer than usual, as if he wanted to make sure they came out as clearly as possible.

"Where's home?" Mrs. Boden asked.

"Argentina," I said in a soft voice.

The adults started talking about Argentina. Ashley Jane yawned loudly, and the baby started fussing.

"We better go," Mrs. Boden said. "Lilly Ann's hungry." The Bodens said goodbye, and I tried to catch Ashley Jane's eye before they walked back across the street, but she never looked in my direction.

My parents chatted excitedly as they walked back in the house, and my brothers and I lingered on the porch for a moment.

"Wow!" Francisco said. "They're super nice!"

"How about we try the cookies?" Mateo asked, and ran inside.

Francisco followed him, and as I was about to trail behind them, I caught my third peek of the little tan dog. It didn't look like it had a collar. Was it a dog that belonged to the whole neighborhood? In our barrio in Mendoza, there were lots of community cats and dogs. The dog saw me too, and we stood looking at each other for a few minutes. I took a step toward it, and it tore off toward the bushes.

"Mimilia, come in! Food!" Mateo shouted.

I ran inside.

CHAPTER 8

The smell of ripe peaches led me back to the fruit bowl in the kitchen. I opted for the soft, fuzzy fruit instead of cookies like my brothers. Juice ran down my chin, and I quickly wiped it with the back of my shirt.

Then I remembered this was my only shirt until my luggage arrived.

Mami shook her head at me as she pulled food from the fridge. Mrs. Campbell had been so thoughtful. I barely registered what I ate, I was so hungry—and because as soon as she'd grabbed a snack, Mami took her laptop out of her backpack to call Lela. The five of us gathered around the computer as the Wi-Fi bars flickered in. Mami signed in to her account.

My heart pounded with each ring.

As soon as I saw Lela's face on the computer screen, my

chin started quivering. Her eyes were watery too, but her smile was radiant.

I had seen her—what?—thirty hours ago? But it felt like a lifetime. I wished I could hug her.

"We made it safe and sound," Papi said.

"Except for Mimilia's luggage," Francisco added, with a look of pity in my direction.

Mami and Papi took turns updating her on everything that had happened since we said goodbye.

"The neighbors are fantastic!" Mami said.

"And look at the kitchen!" Francisco exclaimed. "We have a microwave and a dishwasher! Look, Lela!"

"Don't forget to show her the dryer! It actually dries the clothes, Lela; it doesn't just wring them out!" Mateo said, sounding like those salesmen on late-night TV.

With Papi's help, my brothers carried the computer around so Lela could see every detail of our new house, from the bathrooms to the views from each window. The clock on the microwave blinked 9:00 p.m. and the sky was still lavender.

Lela was the best audience. She gasped at all the right things and clapped and celebrated when she heard they'd already become best friends with two of the Boden boys, whose names were Henry and John-William.

When we reached my room in the attic, Lela said, "Now, boys, you've been the best tour guides. Let me talk to María Emilia for a little bit."

I looked at Papi, and he winked at me and said, "You heard Lela, boys. Let's give the girls some space."

After some protesting, the boys stomped all the way back to the main floor. Papi kissed the top of my head. "I'll be nearby if you need me."

I didn't know what he meant. Of course he'd be nearby. Downstairs. But when I looked at him, he only smiled at me and followed the boys.

Finally in peace, Lela took a deep breath and said, "I'm so glad to see all the blessings you have, Mimilia. Your family. This new house. Your mom's new job. This opportunity. I want you to remember them because I have to tell you some sad news."

My mind went silent, and my whole body tingled as I braced myself. But her expression was heartbreaking, so I promised myself that no matter what she told me, I wouldn't cry in front of her.

"Yesterday, Estrellita crossed the rainbow bridge to cat heaven. When I came home from the airport, she was already gone." Her voice rang in my ears and made them hurt.

It took a moment for the words to make their way to my brain so I could understand them. And when I did, there was no music to help me through the pain. Just two words: *Estrellita's gone!*

"Gone? As in, she left?" I asked. "Maybe she went out through the window in the laundry room again, Lela. Did you check?" A knot of tears grew in my throat. I knew there was no hope.

Lela dried her cheeks with a handkerchief, one that Celestina had made.

"I found her in her bed, curled like a little fur ball. She looked like she was sleeping," Lela said. "It's like she was waiting for you to leave before she could leave too."

I swallowed, but the knot in my throat wouldn't go away. Slowly, I sank onto the side of the bed and gently placed the laptop beside me, Lela's wide, kind eyes blurry across the connection.

The night Lela gave me the binder with Celestina's letters,

I promised her I'd try to make the best of my situation because it was an opportunity, a chance for a better life, not a punishment. Lela expected me to rise above this, losing my cat without saying a final goodbye. But I realized that I had wasted the wish from the shooting star I'd seen that night. I had kept it for the future, thinking that everyone I loved would always be there waiting for me to come back one day. And now Estrellita was gone.

Downstairs, I heard the sound of someone knocking on the door, and I came out of the swirl of emotions. Through the window, I could see that it was finally dark. This day had been the longest in my life.

On the other side of the screen, a world away, Lela looked at me, wrapped in her colorful shawl, waiting for me to collect myself.

"I'm sorry you're all alone, Lela," I said with a shuddering breath.

Lela shook her head. "What are you talking about? Don't I have you in front of me right now? And believe it or not, I feel Estrellita's presence everywhere in the house. Those we love are never far, mi amor."

I knew she was trying to help me feel better, but the distance felt so cruel. I wanted to hug her and mourn the loss of our friend together.

"Now, let me speak with your mami, please," Lela said. "See you tomorrow?"

"See you tomorrow, Lela. Tell Violeta I say hello. Te quiero."

"Te quiero, Mimilia."

I went downstairs, carrying the computer carefully because today had already included too many earth-shattering events for a lifetime. We couldn't afford to lose the only bridge to our family back home.

The kitchen was quiet, and I realized that my brothers must have fallen asleep although it wasn't even ten p.m. A first.

Mami was writing in her journal on the kitchen counter, and I wondered how she'd felt the last few hours, and if she was nervous about her first day at her new job tomorrow.

When she saw me, she gave me a sad smile and rose from her stool. "Are you okay?" she asked. I saw on her face how much she wanted to fix everything for me.

"You knew?"

She nodded. "Lela texted me when we were boarding the flight to Miami. I'm sorry I didn't tell you then."

Papi walked toward us from the boys' room. His eyes were squinty with sleep, and his hair was poking in every direction. He'd been waiting up to make sure I was okay. My heart swelled with love for my parents. Lela was right, and in spite of the sadness, I could see that I was so blessed.

I placed the laptop on the counter, blew a kiss to Lela, and hugged my parents.

"Good night, Mimilia," Papi said. "Tomorrow will be a new and exciting day."

I nodded but, in my heart, I was . . . *bereft.*

That was a word I'd studied for a test but whose meaning I had never really known before now.

I went back to my room in the attic, which was so special and fancy that I felt bad for wishing I was in my room in Mendoza instead, with my cat by my side.

After brushing my teeth, I got under the covers in the same clothes I'd traveled in. The bed was soft and fluffy. The image of my cat, alone as she got ready to leave this world, crushed my heart. But the tears wouldn't come.

I remembered the circular rainbow, the glory, I'd seen from the airplane.

Maybe that had been Estrellita's soul saying goodbye to me? Was it true, what Lela said, that those we love are never far? Even if that was the case, how would Estrellita find me when I was in a whole different country?

I finally knew what wish to make. "I wish for my friend to find her way to me."

Outside, in the glow of the streetlamp, I saw the willow branches dancing to the music of the wind. A dog barked and howled as if it were singing the same songs as the trees. I couldn't help it. Half asleep, I continued writing the song I'd started the day of the English test:

> *The mountain is hard to climb*
> *When you think you're all alone.*
> *In the darkness, the wind blowing,*
> *The doubts are louder,*
> *The fear is stronger.*
> *Just extend your hand and you'll find*
> *Those you love are never far.*

Across oceans, mountains, rivers,

Years or worlds apart,

In spite of death,

Love knows no end.

The bonds can stretch,

But they won't break unless you forget

That those you love are never far.

CHAPTER 9

When I woke up, the room was so dark and quiet it took me a second to remember where I was. The flight, losing my luggage, Mrs. Campbell's visit, the Bodens' welcome, and Lela's news of Estrellita's death came back with a rush.

It hadn't been a nightmare, then.

Last night, I had wished for my kitty to make her way back to me somehow, and I thought I would dream about her. That I'd get a chance to say goodbye for good. But my sleep had been so heavy that I didn't remember dreaming anything.

I tried to imagine what Celestina would have done in my place. I pulled the binder from under my pillow to reread the second letter.

Nonna Rosa,

The seasons here are not the same as back home. It feels like instead of crossing the Atlantic, the boat traveled to another world. Everything is so different. The heat is sticky, and the mosquitoes . . . You wouldn't believe the state of my poor legs. But the fireflies! When I first saw them, I immediately thought of you. They're magical.

The Argentines have a drink called mate that they all love. The first time I sipped it, I didn't know how hot the water would be and it scalded my lips, my tongue, and my throat. I haven't been able to taste any food. Mama had a good laugh about that, but I'm so angry no one warned me. Like they say here, I feel like a toad from another pond, and although I'm surrounded by people, I feel so lonely.

I miss you, dear Nonna.

Love,
Celestina

There were no answers in this letter, but I felt so bad for my great-grandma, not being able to eat anything after she got scalded with the mate. In all my nebulous memories of her, the mate was always her loyal companion. I wondered how long it had taken her to fall in love with it.

I brushed my teeth and tried to comb my hair with my fingers. I wondered if that knock on the door last night had been the airline dropping off my luggage like they'd promised, and I went downstairs in search of food and some needed good news.

Papi was in the kitchen. I could see the island had become the family's gathering place already.

"How are you feeling, pajarita?"

The knot came back to my throat, but I had promised not to cry. Besides, I didn't want to start my first proper day in the United States in a bad way.

"I'm . . . okay," I said. "Just hungry."

"Breakfast is ready for you." He pointed at the doughnuts and hot mate cocido with milk on the counter.

The taste of the familiar tea comforted me, but even though the sugar-dusted doughnut looked tempting, it was too greasy for my taste. I couldn't take more than a bite. Maybe one day like Celestina my taste buds would adjust?

While I finished my tea, I asked, "Did my luggage arrive, Papi?"

"Not yet," Papi said as he wiped the counter. "The airline can't find it, I'm afraid."

I sighed in frustration. Why did the airline have to lose *my* suitcase? It wasn't fair!

As if he could read my thoughts, Papi added, "Last night, the Bodens brought some clothes you can wear in the meantime."

"That's so nice of them!" I said, determining right then to try to win Ashley Jane's friendship. But first, I had to practice saying her name. Ashley Jane. Jane with a *j-j-j*. Not *sh*.

"I still hope I get my suitcase, Pa," I said. "I hadn't worn most of the clothes I packed! They were the ones for the trip to Córdoba and a shirt that Violeta gave me."

"I'm sure it'll turn up," he said.

I could hear the boys chattering in their room but sat up on my stool. "Where's Mami?"

"She's already at the college, signing forms."

I looked at the clock on the wall. It was one.

"Is that clock right?" I asked, blinking and squinting my eyes over and over. "How can it be one p.m.?"

Papi nodded. "Mami waited for you, in case you needed

to talk to her, but she had to leave so she wouldn't be late. Besides, you looked so tired, she didn't want to wake you. Now, how do you feel about going to school to sign you up? Or would you rather stay home?"

I'd rather go back to my home, the real one.

The thought took me by surprise.

Before I could decide how to answer, someone knocked on the door.

"I'll get it!" Mateo said, dashing for the door.

"Maybe it's Henry and John-William again!" Francisco exclaimed, running after him.

My jaw dropped at the way my brother pronounced the *j* in John. Perfectly. Not even twenty-four hours in this country and his accent was already much better than mine. How was this fair?

Mateo and Francisco opened the door. Monserrat was on the other side.

Mrs. Campbell smiled when she saw me.

"How are you feeling?" she asked in Spanish. "Your mami told me about your cat. I'm so sorry."

I sighed, trying to relieve the heaviness in my chest.

Shake it off, shake it off, I sang to myself, and in spite of the sadness, the song still cheered me a bit.

"Pajarita," Papi said, collecting my empty tea mug from the countertop. "Do you want to stay? We can do this tomorrow."

"No, Papi. Let me go change," I said. "I won't be long."

Before heading to my room, I grabbed the bulging plastic bag that sat at the foot of the steep staircase.

Finally! Clean clothes. I rummaged in the bag and found a pair of jeans that were just the right amount of worn in the knees to be fashionable and a T-shirt that said *RED LEDGES BATTLE OF THE BANDS*. It all looked almost new. I couldn't believe the Bodens' generosity.

After a quick shower, I dressed and stood in front of the full-length mirror behind the closet door. The clothes fit me perfectly. But after the months of winter, the trip, and the bad news, I was so pale I looked almost yellow. Dark circles rimmed my eyes.

"Ready to go?" Papi called from the kitchen.

I pinched my cheeks to give them some color and headed downstairs.

"Nice outfit, Mimilia!" Mateo said.

I wasn't sure that a compliment from a six-year-old who still put his shoes on the wrong feet was what I needed, but by this point, I was desperate for some good vibes to boost my confidence.

The boys climbed into the back seat of Mrs. Campbell's car, a small Bug car with a flower-shaped air freshener dangling from the mirror. Papi locked up behind me. In the daytime, our house still looked charming.

At the house across the street, I saw Ashley Jane looking out the window, and I waved. She must have not seen me because she didn't wave back. But then, it seemed like she was looking past me anyhow. I turned to look over my shoulder and saw that same tan dog for the fourth time now. It was sitting under the willow tree. Staring at me, black ears perked in my direction. I suspected it had been waiting for me. But it was such a ridiculous idea that I shooed it away.

I wished I hadn't overslept and wasted the morning. I could've befriended the dog. Or even better, my neighbor.

"Let's go," Francisco urged me. Everyone was looking at me. And when I turned back, the dog wasn't there anymore. I hoped that along with the annoying voice in my mind, I wasn't imagining things.

I got in the car, and Monserrat headed into town.

It was so nice of her to drive us, but I wondered how we'd all get to school. We didn't know anyone we could carpool with. Unless the Bodens . . . but no. Ashley was going into seventh.

We stopped in front of an enormous gray building. At first, I thought it was Mami's college, where she was going to teach, and then I saw the sign that read *Red Ledges Elementary*. I followed Papi and Mrs. Campbell inside, trying to keep my brothers in check and wondering why *red* and *read* were pronounced the same way. The more I learned about English, the less sense it made.

Mrs. Campbell's phone rang, and when she looked at her screen, she tsked. "Miguel, something came up at the college with one of my other international professors."

Papi placed a hand on her shoulder. "I'll take care of this, Montserrat. Don't worry."

"I hate to leave you stranded . . ."

"We'll take the bus," Francisco said. "We take the bus everywhere. Don't we, Mimilia?"

Mrs. Campbell smiled and ruffled his hair. "I know it seems impossible to comprehend, but there are no public buses in Red Ledges. Only school buses."

"How do people get around?" I asked.

"They drive," she said. "The students ride bikes or their scooters. Or they walk."

Mateo's eyebrows rose all the way to his hairline, looking as unconvinced as I felt. He didn't know how to ride a bike yet. The first time he tried, he'd fallen on a rosebush, and he hadn't wanted to do it again. As for me, I felt a pang when I realized that I'd have to depend on being driven around to see my friends—the ones I'd meet soon. As soon as school started.

"How are we getting back home?" I asked.

"I'll be right back," Montserrat said. "Thirty minutes max. Oh! And I'm hoping that my granddaughter Tirzah can meet us later. She said she was on her way."

She kissed us goodbye, and when we walked into the school, I was still soaring with the possibility of meeting a potential friend.

CHAPTER 10

Schools had the same scent of freshly sharpened pencils and new paper everywhere, it seemed.

A woman with beautiful brown curly hair welcomed us.

"New students?" she said, smiling at my brothers, who'd gone skittish as soon as she had seen them.

"Yes, two new students," Papi said.

Mateo looked at me with bright eyes. "I wish we could go here together, Mimilia. This place is way bigger than my kindergarten back home."

Francisco took his hand and said, "Don't worry. I'll protect you."

My heart grew ten sizes. They were so lucky to have each other!

"Welcome to Red Ledges Elementary!" the woman said.

She grabbed a jar with foil-wrapped chocolates and offered it to me. "Take a Kiss, darling."

"Thanks," I said, taking a candy, and passed the container to my brothers.

Papi took a candy too, and armed with a pen he'd brought from Mendoza, he started filling out a stack of papers.

Luckily, in the office there was a saltwater fish tank, and soon my brothers were entranced following Nemo and Dory around.

When I heard kids' voices, I looked up and saw three kids coming down the hallway. Two boys and a girl. One of the boys was tall and thin and had messy light brown hair sticking out in all directions. His jeans were ripped on the knees, and he had a black T-shirt that read *Caifanes*. The other boy had dark skin like mine and curly black hair. He wore a Barcelona jersey and soccer shorts and a smirk on his face that said *troublemaker*. The girl was as tall as the first boy, with freckled light skin, and I definitely recognized her bright red hair from the day before. Today, she wore pink pants and a white shirt with a unicorn on it.

Even though yesterday seemed like a million years ago, this

had to be the three kids who were walking in the middle of the road with the little dog.

Could this girl be Mrs. Campbell's granddaughter?

She and her friends looked so cool. I'd never had any issues making new friends before, but now I felt tongue-tied.

They came in the office, and the secretary broke out in a grin. "Hi, kids. Thanks for visiting me."

The girl went straight for the bowl of chocolates, both boys on her heels. "Of course!"

"Thank you for the Kisses, Mandy!" the boy with the ripped jeans said.

"Yeah, thanks," the other one echoed.

Mandy smiled again. "I know you're going to love middle school, but my days won't be the same without you. What brought you here? My Kisses?"

The girl smiled and flipped her hair over her shoulder. "We came to meet my grandma, but I don't know where she is. Have you s—" Then her eyes fell on me and her face lit up. "Are you the new girl? María?"

Every word in either English or Spanish vanished from my mind. I probably looked like one of the fish—fishes?—in the tank, opening and closing my mouth. The more I tried to rehearse how to start a sentence, the less sense I made.

Then she gave me a small smile that looked like she felt bad for me. My cheeks went hot. "¿Eres la nueva chica? ¿Es tu nombre María?" she said in a similar accent to Mrs. Campbell's. The way she said the *ch* sound reminded me of the TV series from Spain that Violeta and I loved to watch.

I knew it wasn't a big deal that she'd called me María. How would she know I used both first and middle names? But still I couldn't help feeling a rush of annoyance.

Papi sent me a look, and finally, I replied in what I hoped was my best English, "How do you do? I'm María *Emilia* actually. Are you Montserrat's daughter?"

The words sounded so stiff and my accent so . . . *thick*, now my whole body seemed to be in flames.

The girl looked at me encouragingly, but the boy with the Caifanes shirt hid his face behind his hand, and I had the suspicion he was laughing at me. I swallowed my embarrassment and just focused on the girl, who switched to English. "I'm Tirzah. Nice to meet you! We wanted to welcome you at the house, but it got so late and I had to go back home. And yes, I'm Montserrat's *granddaughter*."

I realized my mistake and blushed.

The tall boy was looking at me through narrowed eyes, and when I looked in his direction, he asked in Spanish, "Where are you from? I can't place your accent."

"I'm from Argentina." A little voice reminded me I had an American passport, but I didn't want to get into details.

He scoffed. "Are you sure? You don't sound like you're from Argentina."

I was stunned. It was the first time in my life my identity had been challenged.

Maybe he sensed how offended I felt because he shrugged and said, "My mom and I love the Argentinian telenovelas, and my dad is a rock en español aficionado, and you sound nothing like the Argentinians—"

"It's *Argentines*," I said, putting a hand up to stop him. I knew Argentinian or even Argentinean was correct too, but I didn't like the way they sounded. *Argentine*—rhymes with *valentine*—sounded way better. "You mean I don't sound like a porteña, someone from Buenos Aires. But I know where I was born and raised. In any case, I say I'm from Argentina, and who are you to suggest I'm not? Where are you from by the way?"

He raised his chin and said, "I'm from Mexico. Any problems with that?"

"Why would I have a problem with that? But how would you feel if I said you don't sound like El Chavo del Ocho? Of course people from the same country have different accents. Like Tirzah speaks like she's from Spain, and she sounds different from my second cousin Cecilia, who lives in Las Islas Canarias. Does that make her any less Spanish?"

He glared at me and started saying something, but Tirzah cut in. "It's okay, Donovan." Then she smiled in my direction and said, "Actually, I'm from Brazil. My whole family is. I have an accent from Spain because of Duolingo."

I had felt so energized arguing in Spanish, but I deflated at having assumed something about Tirzah myself. Why did I have to be so confrontational with the first kids my age I'd met?

"Beto is from Nicaragua," Tirzah said, and the other boy waved at me, bobbing his head up and down. I thought he was greeting me until I saw the two thin cables of his headphones. "He moved here two years ago. We used to have Lucas in our group. He was born in Uruguay but grew up in Italy. He moved to Salt Lake over the summer."

Beto kept nodding at me, but Donovan was looking at my brothers, who were still mesmerized by the fish.

There was an awkward silence, and then my dad exclaimed, "I'm done!" He handed the papers to Mandy, who had been following our conversation in Spanish like she was a spectator at a tennis match.

Mandy read the forms and documents Papi had brought. Birth certificates and passports, vaccine and school records.

"Francisco?" she called.

My little brother whipped around and said, "Here!"

Then she called, "Mateo!"

Never one to stay behind, Mateo said, "Here!"

His little pinched face made my heart quiver. They may have had better accents than me, but starting at a new school was going to be hard for all of us.

Papi and Mandy talked about how there were openings in both first and second grade in the Spanish immersion program. I translated the news to my brothers in a whisper, aware of Tirzah's and her friends' curious looks. But I only had eyes for Mateo's relieved expression.

"We'll be in the same class as the neighbor boys!" Francisco whisper-shouted.

Before we left, Mandy gave my brothers each another chocolate Kiss. Donovan and Beto helped themselves too, and Mandy said, "Come see me again soon!"

"We will," they replied in unison.

Outside, Mrs. Campbell was already waiting for us by the curb.

"Avó!" Tirzah called, and ran to hug her grandma. I missed Lela with the intensity of a million suns, and perhaps for the first time in my life I understood what it meant to feel sick with jealousy.

"Everything went okay?" Mrs. Campbell asked Papi. Now her Portuguese accent seemed unmistakable. How hadn't I recognized it before?

Papi gave her a short recap, and she sighed. "Well, at least two out of my errands today went right."

"What was the other one?" Tirzah asked.

Mrs. Campbell sighed again. "Missing luggage." Hope

flared in me, but she said, "No news of yours yet, María Emilia. I'm sorry."

I sagged. At least I had met Tirzah. Maybe we could hang out together this week before school started. It would be great to practice English with her, and—

My plans tumbled like a house of cards when I heard her say, "We're leaving in an hour, Avó. I'll see you next week." She kissed her grandma and turned to leave. But then, as if she remembered I was standing there, hoping for a crumb of friendship, she turned around and said, "See you on the first day of school, María Emilia!"

"Where are you going?" The words blurted out before I could stop them. I sounded so desperate, but how did the saying go? Desperate times call for desperate decisions, or something like that. I wanted to seem cool, but most of all, I didn't want to be lonely.

Donovan and Beto were already walking ahead, and Tirzah replied, "My family is going camping. I'll be back the night before the first day of school. I'll see you later!"

She and the boys left before I could say anything else.

CHAPTER 11

Downcast, I got into the back seat and stayed quiet on the way to my future school. Papi and Montserrat talked about school buses.

"I've always wanted to ride in one," Mateo whispered to me.

"It will be like in the movies," Francisco added. "Right, Mimilia?"

"Yes," I said, and I wasn't even lying.

By the way things were going, I dreaded that, for me, school would be like a scary movie, but my brothers didn't need to know that.

My building was twice as big as the elementary school. The sign said *Red Ledges Middle School*.

As we walked in, I wondered what *middle* meant. I'd

expected it to be called a high school like I'd heard. Instead of the comforting smell of pencils and paper, there was an unfamiliar scent that I could only guess was old cafeteria food.

I followed Mrs. Campbell and Papi closely. My brothers held on to my shirt as we walked through hallways full of people. There were posters and signs advertising chess, robotics, LEGO clubs.

"What extracurricular activities would you like to do?" Papi asked me. "Something to do with music? Perhaps you could learn to play an instrument?"

Although my parents had wanted my brothers and me to learn an instrument, our budget was stretched to the max with my English lessons, which they always picked for me first. This was a new possibility.

I'd always liked the idea, but now a certain poster caught my eye. The school looked like those in the movies, and if there was anything I'd learned in twelve years of TV education, it was that the way to have more friends was to become a cheerleader.

Visions of me in a cute uniform, waving pom-poms, flashed in my mind.

"Cheer?" I said. "They sing for the school teams, right?"

"That would be a fantastic way to meet people!" Mrs. Campbell said, and I felt proud of my decision.

When we found the main office and saw it was packed with people, Mateo exclaimed, "Are you kidding me?" His words echoed everyone's feelings.

Mrs. Campbell said, "Why don't I wait outside on the front lawn with the boys? I think I have a ball in the trunk of my car."

I breathed a sigh of relief.

"You're a lifesaver, Montserrat," Papi said. "Thank you!"

"My pleasure!" she said, and holding my brothers' hands, headed out.

I got in the back of the line while Papi picked out the right forms at the counter. I slowly printed what I knew and handed it to Papi for the parts I didn't. By the time we finished, we were at the front.

"Good afternoon," said a woman with colorful glasses hanging from a chain on her neck. A little plaque on the counter read *Cindy*. "Let me see your forms." She perched her glasses on the tip of her nose and scanned the papers. "Oh, honey," she exclaimed in a sad voice. "I'm sorry. The cheer squad was selected last month." Cindy frowned, but then she added cheerfully, "But there are way more options than cheer. You don't have to make a decision today, okay?"

"Okay, thanks," I said, my visions vanishing in a puff.

After making copies of my passport and vaccine records, she handed me a printout of my schedule and a gray T-shirt with the logo of a . . . ball of fire?

"Here's your schedule, love. Welcome to Red Ledges! We're happy to have you as our newest Meteor!"

"Meteor? That's an original school mascot," Papi said.

While they dove into a detailed conversation about the tourists that came to the Utah desert to gaze at stars and other celestial bodies, I glanced at the schedule. My name was listed as María E. Soler. I tried not to let that bother me. But my stomach dropped when I saw the top of the paper said seventh grade.

"Excuse me, Ms. Cindy," I said, trying to sound as respectful as possible. "But there's a mistake. I'm going into eighth grade . . . In Argentina, I was almost done with seventh! I'm supposed to be at the high school. And also, I already speak English."

"But according to your records, you haven't had any US or Utah history, María. Here, students don't switch to the high school building until tenth grade, anyway." *That's* what *middle* meant. It sure was starting to feel like being stuck in the middle. "And as far as ELL class, it's policy for all our immigrant students to take it, no matter what level they're at," she said.

Perhaps I was being a little disrespectful, but I slid my blue American passport toward her.

She blinked a few times. "Technically you're not an immigrant . . . but you're still an English learner."

I turned to Papi so he'd intervene for me. "Repeat seventh grade?" I said a little too loudly. "I've never repeated anything in my life! I was at the top of my class back home."

Why was everything going wrong just for me? Was I wishing for the wrong thing over and over?

Cindy started explaining to Papi that without a certificate that said I'd completed seventh grade there was nothing else she could do. I wanted to understand her, but right then, a cluster of girls stood behind us in line.

"She has to repeat seventh grade," one of the girls whispered to the others.

I turned toward them to clarify the misunderstanding and came face-to-face with Ashley Jane Boden, my neighbor.

"Hi, Ashley Jane!" I said, forcing a smile, but as soon as her name passed my lips, I cringed. The *j* had sounded more like a *ch*! I'd called her . . . *chain*. She didn't look impressed.

Before I could apologize, one of her friends pointed at me and asked, "Isn't that your favorite shirt, AJ?"

Another one added, "Who is she? Why is she wearing your shirt?"

Ashley Jane—AJ?—glared at me. She shook her head and said, "That's where my shirt is." I looked at the T-shirt I'd been so grateful to have this morning, and I realized that the words were formed by dozens of people's names. My eyes zeroed in on *Ashley Jane Boden*. This was a team shirt. My neighbor continued. "I can't believe my mom would give it to you without asking me first. I should pay more attention to what she puts in the hand-me-downs box."

"My mom did that the other day," her friend added. "It's

a bummer when they donate clothes to the poor without asking first."

Usually, Violeta wore the clothes I grew out of because I was a little chunkier and taller than she was. And I bought a lot of things secondhand because the situation in Argentina, especially after my mom lost her job, was really hard. But I'd never considered my cousin or myself *poor*. In my family we never lacked for anything, but for the first time I wondered if, compared to our neighbors in Red Ledges, we were poor.

My parents had taught me that the value of a person can't be measured by what they wore or what they owned. I'd never doubted before. But now, the way AJ and her friends looked at me, how they'd said *hand-me-downs*, I felt like I'd shrunk two sizes.

"Why is she just looking at us?" one of them said. "Doesn't she talk?"

Ashley Jane threw her dark brown hair over her shoulder. "Don't worry about her, Kel. She doesn't really speak English."

They walked away quickly, pretending I wasn't still standing there, clutching the meteor shirt close to my chest and rehearsing in my mind a million comebacks I didn't know how to phrase.

"Let's go, María Emilia," Papi said. "It's all fixed."

Hope fluttered in my heart. "Am I going into eighth, then?"

Papi shook his head. "No, mi amor. But it'll be for the best. You'll see."

Too disappointed to keep arguing, I followed him outside.

I got into the car first, sulky, and Mateo and Francisco joined me in the back seat, sweaty, stinky, and happy from kicking the ball around with other kids their age. No. Not happy. They were *exhilarated*.

"This has been the best day of my life," Mateo said.

Francisco added, "I love this country." He sighed contentedly, waving goodbye to his new friends.

Somewhere on the way from our new house to the middle school, the ground had opened up underneath my feet, swallowed me, and spit out a different version of me.

My life was not the glamourous adventure I'd imagined. I'd had so many expectations, and my parents and Lela hoped for so many things from me, but I was already letting them down before school even started.

I'd been born in the United States, and even though I spoke English, it still wasn't good enough. If only my tongue and my lips would pronounce things the proper way, then maybe AJ wouldn't hate me so much.

As soon as we arrived at the house, I ran upstairs and took off the T-shirt that had been Ashley Jane's. I felt like I'd stolen from her. I put on one of Mami's shirts instead.

I spent some time finally writing out a message to Violeta, about her shirt being missing in my lost luggage, the seventh grade/middle school news, and, most of all, Ashley Jane. I couldn't wait for Violeta's reply. I could picture her reaction! But imagining the expressions on her face made me miss her even more.

When Mami came home from work, she had a radiant smile on her face. A coworker had helped her find an affordable car to buy.

We'd never had a car before!

"Hola, mi amor. How are you feeling? How was your day? And why are you wearing my *one* workout shirt? Didn't you find anything you liked in the bag the Bodens brought?"

I'd hoped to unburden my heart with her, tell her all about AJ and her awful friend Kel. About having to repeat seventh grade. But I didn't want to ruin her day.

"No. There was nothing that fit," I lied. "I'm sorry for wearing your shirt, Mami. I'll give it back once I've washed my *one* outfit." My voice sounded way sassier than I'd intended, but it felt better than sadness.

My mom pressed her lips, and after a deep breath, she brushed a hand over my hair and said, "No news of your luggage, eh? I know it's hard, but a little more patience, mi amor."

Patience wasn't my specialty. After the rice and meatballs Papi made for dinner, I sat by the window to watch for the airport shuttle that would bring me back my few possessions from Mendoza. If my life were a movie, this would be the part with the sad piano music.

As the sun went down, my heart drummed painfully in my chest, chanting that Red Ledges Middle School was a big place to be in without a friendly face.

CHAPTER 12

The next few days went by with no sign of my lost luggage. Violeta wrote back, and we exchanged updates. I tried to write music as I watched for the airport shuttle out the window, but the lyrics that had come so naturally on the airplane sounded empty to my ears.

Those who loved me, my family, were right next to me, but they weren't facing the same mountain I was. As AJ and her friends played with my brothers in their front yard, I wished I had the courage to cross the street and ask those girls to give me another chance. If only Tirzah, Montserrat's granddaughter, hadn't gone on a trip!

No wish on a shooting star could help me make friends before school started. I hadn't even seen the little stray dog again although I'd waited for it by the willow tree every day.

And every night, I missed little Estrellita's warmth next to me.

The boys spent the last day before school in the Bodens' pool while I cooked to death in my attic room. That evening, Francisco asked, "How come you don't sing anymore, Mimilia? Are you sad?"

"I'm not sad!" I snapped at him, and he recoiled.

I immediately wanted a do-over. I wasn't sad, but I was worried and scared.

"Why is she so mean?" Francisco asked Mateo.

Mateo shrugged and whispered, "She's almost a teenager. Leave her alone . . ."

I hated that my brothers were scared of me. What had happened to me in just a few days?

Not only had my life turned upside down, but I felt like I was a different person. One I didn't really like. Worse, one my family didn't like. How were other people going to like me if my own family couldn't stand me?

My brothers kept whispering about me, and I stomped back to my room to prepare my outfit for tomorrow. I figured that everyone would wear the meteor shirt on the first day, in an act of unity since there weren't uniforms here. I absolutely refused to wear any of the clothes Mrs. Boden had given me, and my parents had seemingly given up on my luggage completely. So Mami had finally agreed to buy me a few things at Walmart. There was one in Mendoza, but it hadn't sold cute shirts or jeans like this one. I might not have had friends, but at least I'd start school with nice-looking clothes that *weren't hand-me-downs*.

My school's first bell rang a whole hour earlier than my brothers' and Mami's first classes, at seven thirty a.m. I'd never attended morning school, and the night before I hardly slept a wink for fear of sleeping in.

I shouldn't have worried. My brothers were up at sunrise, too excited to stay in bed. As they and Mami finished getting ready, Papi snapped a few pictures to send Lela, and then he sent me off. From the window, he watched me as I headed to the school bus stop. I walked behind Ashley Jane and her friends the whole way. After one glance in my direction, they laughed like they'd seen the funniest thing in the world.

Luckily the bus arrived quickly. Would it be like on TV, like I told my brothers? My heart sank when I realized no one else was wearing the meteor school T-shirt. Ashley Jane and her friends sat at the front, and I walked toward the middle where there was an empty row.

Maybe the girls were laughing at my outfit. I tried to ignore them, but between my embarrassment, the chaos, and the odd smell, I wished they'd held me back two years instead of one. At least I'd be in the same school as my brothers.

I spent the bus trip fantasizing that Tirzah and I were friends, gossiping together. I hoped to find her in my classes.

When the bus arrived at school, the building loomed ominously even though the morning was a bright blue that contrasted against the red rock of the canyon. The temperature was already so high, I worried I'd get sweat stains under my armpits.

Although I had my schedule in front of my eyes, the building was a big and crowded maze.

When I found my math class, everyone was seated and the teacher was already reviewing the course objectives. She gave me a tiny nod while I tried to come up with an excuse for being late. But she didn't stop talking, and I snaked around the edges of the room, trying to find an empty spot. I didn't understand everything she said, but when I saw the material we'd be studying, I sighed in relief. I'd already gone over negative numbers and probabilities at school in Mendoza, so this class wouldn't be so hard.

After I'd calmed down enough to absorb my surroundings, I saw most of my classmates had calculators right there on their desks, out in the open, without even trying to hide them from the teacher.

My heart jumped to my throat when I noticed Tirzah was in my class. To my surprise, she was wearing the school meteor T-shirt too, except hers had a sticker above the fireball. It was the head of an astronaut. No! Not a normal astronaut. A dog astronaut!

When I was about to wave at her, the teacher called, "María Soler?"

At first, I didn't understand that she was calling my name because she'd put emphasis on the first syllable and added so much r-sound, making it sound like *SOH-lerr*. My last name wasn't *Solar*! But when no one raised their hand, she looked at me and lowered her glasses to take a better look.

Tirzah made a head signal for me to reply, and I said, "Oh, me? It's María Emilia Soler. So-LER."

I don't know why the rest of the kids laughed. I hadn't said anything funny, had I? Did my name have a secret meaning I didn't know? Papi had warned me that some words had different meanings in other languages.

I felt the heat rising all the way to the top of my head.

The teacher had put a mark on the paper and moved on. I hoped it wasn't a sign that meant I was a troublemaker. I'd never had any behavioral issues in my life before.

But to make matters worse, she announced a quiz, and my hands prickled with sweat even though the room was freezing. In Mrs. Prescott's class, a quiz had been a big deal, a test. I took a notebook and a pencil out of my backpack and waited for instructions. But when everyone went to the back of the class to grab a tablet, I wondered if I was in the wrong class. Tablets in math?

I stayed in my seat, the only student to do so, and the teacher looked at me with a question in her eyes.

She said something, and when I didn't reply, she repeated it louder. Everything in my brain shut down. She could've asked me my name, and I wouldn't have been able to answer.

Tirzah was walking back in my direction with a tablet in

each hand, and before my tongue got unstuck, she placed one on my desk.

I'd played with Mami's iPad sometimes, but I'd never seen this kind of tablet before. I didn't even know how to turn it on.

Around me, the rest of the class knew what to do and got to work right away.

The teacher stared at me until her eyes widened, and she said, "Oh, you're the new student from Argentina." She looked around the room, and when she saw Tirzah, she asked, "Tirzah, please can you help her?"

Tirzah looked back at her tablet, and after a second, she put it down and headed toward me.

Quietly, she sat next to me and showed me how to get to the math app. "Enter your student number and passcode," she said. "Then you'll be able to access your test."

I nodded, and she went back to her seat before I realized she'd spoken in Spanish.

My heart overflowed with gratitude for her. She had lost precious time working on her test to help me. True, the teacher had asked her to, but she did it without complaint. I wanted to dive into my math problems. Instead, in my mind

I paddled in an ocean of confusion, trying to figure out what my student number or passcode was. There was no way I'd interrupt Tirzah again. Just before I gave in and drowned in desperation, a little light went on in my mind.

Would those numbers be on the schedule the school secretary had given me? I took the paper out of my pocket, and I scanned the form as fast as I could. And there, in the upper-left corner, was all my information. I entered the numbers as quickly as I could, but there was no passcode.

I sighed, crushed that I'd have to tell the teacher I needed help after all. But Tirzah, who was looking at me from her seat next to the window, whispered loud enough for me to catch her words: "Last four digits of your student number."

My fingers typed the number in, and finally, I was logged on.

The clock had swept forward without mercy. By the time I went through the first five problems, the bell rang.

A part of my brain kept working feverishly while my fingers typed, and the other was aware of the teacher pointing at the back of the room and saying, "Log off your tablets and place them back on the shelves. I'll hand out reports next time we meet."

Sweat exploded in my armpits. I didn't even know how many questions there were on the test! I couldn't make a basic calculation to estimate how bad my grade would be. But one thing was certain: It would definitely be bad.

Kids were leaving, and others were coming. I wanted to catch up to Tirzah and thank her for her help, but first, I had to fix this.

The chair made a horrible scraping sound when I got up to talk to the teacher. It was one thing to be shy and self-conscious about my accent, but quite another to let my first day of school be a disaster because I wasn't willing to speak up.

"Excuse me," I said, folding my arms to hide that my hands were shaking.

The teacher's eyes were a cloudy green when she looked at me, waiting for me to speak.

"Professor, I've never used a tablet at school before, and I didn't know my sign-in information. My report won't be good—" My voice started quavering, and before I embarrassed myself by bursting into tears, I swallowed my words.

She must have taken pity on me because her expression

softened. "Listen, María." I must have made a face because she added, "It's María, right?"

I shook my head. "María Emilia."

She chuckled. "That's too long!"

I'd never thought about my name being long. Ashley Jane was the same length as mine, and other than her friend calling her AJ, no one else seemed to have a problem with it.

The teacher was talking, and I yanked myself back to the present. I had to look at her lips to make sense of what she was saying. She spoke too fast.

". . . an assessment. A way to see how quickly students find their legs coming back to school after a long summer recess."

"But I didn't have a recess," I said. "I was at school two weeks ago."

She chuckled again as if I'd told a joke, but I was dead serious.

Students were coming in for the next class.

The teacher looked over my shoulder. "Don't worry too much about it. Now you know for the next time."

That wasn't the answer I expected. I wanted to do the test

over, but the bell rang again, and when I looked back, all the seats were filled. It was too late to ask.

"You should be in your next class," she said, making a shooing gesture with her hand. "Now run along. We can talk about it next time."

I hoisted my backpack on my shoulder and left the classroom, aware that everyone was looking at me.

In the deserted hallway, there was no trace of Tirzah or any friendly face. As I peered at the printout of the map to find the science lab, I had the foolish impulse to run away. The clock on top of the lockers thundered in my ears, or maybe it was my galloping heart. Time in the Northern Hemisphere was running faster than below the equator, and I tried to race it to the other end of the building.

When I arrived at the lab, late, I was gasping for air. I'd never had a male teacher before in my life. I was instantly intimidated.

The teacher looked up at me and shook his head. "I'll forgive you this time because it's the first day, but there won't be any more exceptions."

"Oh," I said, my face burning. "I thought this class started at half past eleven."

He tilted his head to the side and narrowed his eyes. "You mean eleven thirty?"

Some people laughed. Maybe I should've run away after all.

I found my seat and tried to guess what the class had been talking about. There was no trace of Tirzah here either. By the time I understood they were talking about forces of physics, the bell rang again.

Jerked out of orbit, I followed the jet stream of students until, somehow, I ended up in English. The ELL class.

Finally, I was on time, but my head was throbbing with the effort to understand what was going on around me. I'd never spoken only in English for so long in my life. Also, my stomach started growling loudly. Breakfast had been a long time ago, but how could I explain that to the boys next to me, who laughed when they looked in my direction? They'd been in my physics class.

I knew I had to ignore them. Once this bout of shyness left me, I'd be back to my assertive self.

But if first impressions make a mark, I was worried this nightmarish first day of school in the United States would leave me friendless.

While we were supposed to read, my mind drifted far, far away. I wondered what Violeta and our friends were doing at school. They had English today. Would Nahuel ask if she had any news from me?

What did Lela do all day long now that we were gone? Did she miss us? I didn't have to wonder about that. I knew she did.

Finally, the bell rang again, and I followed my classmates down to the cafeteria. Today had been nothing like I had imagined. I never saw a single person twice. I'd never caught another glimpse of Tirzah. How many students were in this school, and how would I ever make a friend?

Although I was hungry, I didn't think I could eat the pasta and meatballs, or the snacks available in the buffet. I grabbed a sandwich from the line and an apple. I found an empty seat at the biggest round table I'd ever seen. It was so big, it was impossible to talk to anyone that wasn't on my left or right, so I didn't even try. I was exhausted. I took a bite of my sandwich, and I almost gagged. The bread was soggy, and the cheese had a plasticky taste. My appetite died.

A knot in my throat choked me. Would everything I ate

here be disgusting? Why was every word that came out of my mouth somehow wrong? I was so sad, my eyes had filled with tears.

"Are you okay?" a soft voice said next to me. The voices and sounds from the cafeteria had blurred into a drone and I hadn't been able to distinguish a single voice, but this one spoke Spanish.

I looked up so fast one of the tears escaped and ran down my cheek before I could stop it. I wiped my face with the back of my hand. Tirzah looked at me with a worried expression.

She was with the same two boys from the elementary school. The accent policer and the boy with headphones both wore the school mascot shirt. But theirs also had the dog astronaut sticker added near the flaming meteor. The boys didn't look at me, as if they couldn't wait to leave for whatever else was more interesting than a lonely girl crying in the school cafeteria on the first day of school.

How had my life come to this? I hadn't even cried on my first day of three-year-old preschool! But I'd never been so lonely before. So out of place.

I remembered Celestina's name for this feeling: being "a

toad from another pond." I identified so much with her—a girl who'd been born almost a hundred years before me.

"Do you need help finding your next class?" Tirzah asked. "I tried to wait for you after math, but a hallway monitor almost wrote me off."

The kindness of her gesture melted the stress that had weighed me down the last few days.

I hadn't complained—that much—when my parents announced the move. Or when the airline lost my suitcase or I found out I'd be repeating seventh grade. I had held my temper when I didn't know the information to log on to the tablet and had done so badly on the math test. Even when the teacher told me off for being late, I had only tried to explain myself.

Yes, I'd cried at how disgusting the sandwich was, but in my defense, I was hungry and tired. My school in Mendoza was only from one to five thirty. I'd been at this horrible school forever, and I was hungry.

I took out the schedule from my pocket. "Do you know where PE Dance is?"

"It's at the end of the hallway," she said, pointing ahead.

"Come on, T!" Donovan said in English, as if I couldn't

understand him. "You don't have to babysit her. She can find her own way, like we all did when we first arrived."

"Did your grandma assign you to help a newbie again?" Beto asked.

Tirzah blushed and shrugged. "No, not really."

Assigned? So she'd been helping me because she'd been asked? I felt so bad I couldn't even look her in the eye.

"Just because she speaks Spanish, the teachers are always asking her to translate and help out the newcomers," Donovan told me, that infuriating smirk back on his face.

"Is that how she met you?" I asked in English.

He scoffed, but I could tell he was surprised I had understood what he'd said.

The bell rang.

"Let's go," Beto said. "We're going to be late."

They went their way, and I went mine, vowing not to talk to any of them again.

But before I went into the dance studio, I looked back and envied them for having each other. Would the boys convince Tirzah not to be friends with me?

CHAPTER 13

Finally, it was the end of the school day. Maybe it was my complete exhaustion, but to me, the buses all looked the same. The drivers all looked the same. All the people looked the same. I didn't recognize a single marker that told me which bus I needed to take back home. But if I didn't get on a bus in the next couple of minutes, I'd be stranded at school forever.

Although there were no sharks for hundreds of miles, ominous music started drumming in my brain.

Looking at the remaining kids on the sidewalk, I caught sight of my neighbor sitting by the window of one of the buses—right as the engine rumbled to life.

"Ashley Jane!" I called. This time, her name came out of my lips as *Ach-lee Yane*. She turned her back toward the window.

And could I really blame her when I was slaughtering her name every single time?

I ran after the bus, waving my hand, but it drove away all the same.

I might as well have been invisible.

Bus after bus left the parking lot.

Breathless, I stood on the sidewalk, without a clue of what to do.

What if I had to stay at school for the rest of my life and my family forgot all about me? I'd be wearing the same outfit, eating the same gross cafeteria sandwiches, all alone for eternity.

"Do you need help?" a boy asked behind me.

I turned around and came face-to-face with the accent-police boy—Donovan.

"Did your bus just leave?" he asked in Spanish.

I nodded.

He sucked air in. "Ooh. That's never fun. What's your address?"

With horror, I realized I had no idea.

I wished I could dissolve into thin air so he couldn't see my embarrassment.

Then I remembered the crumpled schedule in my pocket. There on the upper-left corner was all my information. But I couldn't make sense of the numbers and letters.

Like a kindergartner, I handed Donovan the paper. He read in silence.

At least no one I knew and cared about was here to see my humiliation.

Donovan shook his head. "Your bus is the rabbit one. It's already gone."

"I know that. Thank you," I said, my voice harsher than I intended. What I really had wanted to ask was: Rabbit?

Donovan must have read my mind because he said, "It has a picture of a rabbit on the windshield. One has a mermaid. Another a dog. Et cetera. Like I said though, yours is the rabbit."

"Oh," I said, angry at myself for not having noticed.

"Do you need a ride?" he asked. "My brother, Julián, can drive you." He pointed at a silver car where a boy who looked like an older version of Donovan was waiting.

My mouth about fell open. "Is he old enough to drive?"

My face must have looked super funny because Donovan laughed. "Julián is eighteen, for your information."

"Oh." I cringed.

"Honestly, Julián's a good driver."

I considered my chances. Even if I called home, how was Papi going to come get me? Mami drove the car, and her workday didn't end until much later.

I didn't want to get in the car of a boy I didn't know. But I couldn't stay at school forever waiting to be rescued!

In Mendoza, we walked everywhere when our bus card didn't have any credit. I had two strong legs, and I'd at least realized the streets in Red Ledges were in a grid.

"What's the address here?" I asked, looking around for a marker that would tell me which way to go.

Donovan shrugged. "Why?" Before I could reply, he called out to his brother in English, "Yo, Jul. What's the address here?"

Julián made the same skeptical expression as Donovan. "Why?"

"To see if I can walk home," I said. "This paper says I live on 743 North, 400 West."

Julián's eyes went wide like flying saucers. "You can't walk that far."

My feathers were ruffled, as Lela would say. "Of course, I can. It's not that far."

Julián shrugged. "The problem is you'd have to go under the overpass. I mean, it's sunny and nice, but that's a deserted area. I wouldn't let Donovan go that way on his own. Either call your parents or let us drive you. I promise we're responsible."

Just then, Donovan finished chugging down a bottle of chocolate milk and burped. He wiped his mouth with the back of his hand and said, "We are."

The car wasn't new, but it looked okay. If I accepted their offer, they could drop me off a block away from my house. My parents need never know I'd ridden home with two strangers. Boys at that. But then, I never lied to my parents. At least not like this, for something important.

"I don't know," I said, looking at the deserted parking lot as if a bus would magically materialize.

"Come on. I have something to do," Donovan said, eyeing his brother. "I can't be late."

I imagined waiting until it got dark. My worried father finding me in the parking lot.

I needed a break from feeling like a hot mess.

"Okay," I finally said, opening the door and sitting in the back seat and making a point of clicking my seat belt. "Please drive safely."

"As you wish!" Julián said, and we took off.

My heart drummed loud in my ears. When nausea started rising, I wondered if it was because I was hungry or nervous or because the back of the car smelled like boys' socks. Maybe all the above.

Julián turned around to look at me and said, "Where are you from?"

Donovan smacked him in the arm and said in English, "She just moved from Argentina. If you're thinking her accent sounds funny, I'm warning you—"

"You know I can understand everything you say, right? I have an accent, but my ears work perfectly well."

Donovan cringed, and his brother shook his head. "I know this guy from Argentina. Tell me what it's like where you live."

The rest of the way home I gave them a little overview of my country, and especially Mendoza. They had no idea Aconcagua, the largest peak in the Western and Southern Hemispheres, was in Argentina.

"I always thought it was in the Himalayas," Donovan said.

I was horrified, feeling an irrational ownership over the cerro I'd seen from my rooftop on sunny days in the valley. A wave of nostalgia swept over me. I'd only been in the United States for a few days, but I missed Mendoza and my life there with a force that made tears prickle my eyes.

Luckily, by then we'd arrived at my house. My little brothers were playing on the porch.

"Oh!" Julián said. "You live in the Jensens' house. I always loved that big round window."

Just then, my dad walked out of the house, phone at his ear. His face relaxed when he saw me, and he hung up.

"Oh no," Donovan said. "Is your dad going to be mad at us?"

Julián parked by the curb, and my dad walked toward the driver's side of the car.

My dad didn't even look angry, but my hands started shaking. I got out of the car and walked to his side.

"Hi, I'm Miguel Soler," he said, and extended his hand for Julián to shake.

"I'm Julián, and this is my brother, Donovan."

Then my dad looked at me. "What happened? We waited at the bus stop, and we panicked when we didn't see you."

"I couldn't find my bus, Papi. I'm sorry. I didn't know what to do, and they offered to help."

Papi's face softened. "Thank you for driving her," he said.

"You're welcome, sir," said Julián.

Donovan smiled tightly at my dad, but he looked relieved. Like he'd expected to get into trouble for doing a good deed, and now that he wasn't, he didn't know how to act.

Papi asked them where they lived, and after a few minutes, the boys drove away.

"Is that your boyfriend?" Francisco asked me in a little voice, his face the image of malice.

Mateo started chanting, "Mimilia has a boyfriend!"

I sent both of them a look meant to stun them into silence. But the ability to correct my brothers seemed to have been lost on the flight to the United States too because they shrugged and left me standing on the sidewalk.

"You should've called me first, María Emilia." Papi's tone was soft, but my insides twisted in shame. "Remember the same rules from back home apply here too because this is home now."

It was one thing to get in trouble at school, to get a bad score, or to sit alone during lunch. Losing my brothers' respect was worrying, but my dad being disappointed in me? What would my mom say when she came back? And when Lela found out?

That was something I couldn't take.

My head starting throbbing. I should've asked Donovan to let me use his phone. I shouldn't have let them drive me without asking my dad if it was okay. I'd have never gotten inside a car with people I didn't know back in Mendoza.

"I tried to be responsible, like you expect me to. You—"

"Mimilia has a boyfriend," my brothers were chanting and clapping. It was in Spanish, but I didn't want anyone to hear them.

"Stop it!" I yelled.

At first, they were stunned. But then Mateo started crying. Francisco looked at me as if I'd become a witch.

Feeling a prickly sensation in the back of my head, I looked up and saw Ashley Jane staring out her window. She hid behind her curtains.

"Emilia, apologize to your brother," my dad said, but I was already stomping inside the house.

CHAPTER 14

When my mom returned home from work, she wasn't happy I'd ridden in a boy's car. A strange boy. But she didn't say very much to me.

Before bed, I crept down to the kitchen to tell her what had really happened at school and paused when I heard her speaking with Lela on the computer.

"I never expected *her* of all of us to hate it so much here," Mami said. "The neighbor next door is adorable. Emilia never had a hard time making the right kind of friends. Why would she start now? She even refuses to wear the clothes they brought over. Everything's practically brand-new."

Quietly, I made my way back upstairs. The Bodens were nice, but AJ was horrible to me. I'd never disliked a person so much before, but thinking back on her ignoring me when I was running after the bus, *dislike* was too soft a word for what I felt.

But Mami wouldn't hear a bad word about her new friend's daughter. She and Mrs. Boden, Stacy, spent a lot of time together after school. And so did my dad with Scott. My brothers practically lived across the street, but I refused to walk into their house even if my nemesis wasn't there.

The week went from bad to worse. Tirzah didn't sit with me at lunch. The only person I really spoke to was my teacher, Mrs. Contreras, for my English Language Learner class, ELL. True to her name, she always had a contradiction ready for anything I said.

While my brothers had a wonderful time at school, speaking Spanish for half the day, for me each subject and period was a torture. Cindy, the school secretary, called me into the office because I hadn't declared a club yet, and if I didn't choose one by the end of the month, I'd be placed in one randomly.

The math teacher, whose name was Mrs. Garcia, didn't help my anxiousness. She had let me retake the test, but the second time around I hadn't done much better.

In fact, my grade had been a perfect zero.

"You need to save your answers before you go to the next screen," the teacher said.

I was appalled. "I never knew . . . Did everything get erased, then?"

The teacher nodded, and I wanted to disappear—just as my answers to the math problems apparently had.

At the end of the day, I got moved to a different math class for English learners even though the language wasn't the problem. It was the technology.

After the class switch, I didn't see Tirzah, Donovan, or Beto. Which was for the best. Donovan had wanted to help, but my parents had been mad at me and my life went upside down.

How unfair that the teachers had never met me at my best! I'd never been the troublemaker, the child my parents worried about. What was wrong with this new María Emilia? I didn't know how to be the girl that made them proud anymore.

To avoid attracting any attention to my struggles, by Friday I had become so quiet I couldn't even remember what it was like to talk to someone who wasn't my family. I even stopped talking with Lela for fear she'd see through the mask I put on every morning to hide how lonely I was.

Each day my heart crumbled more with the need to talk to someone, anyone.

I read Celestina's letters more often, but she hadn't written to her grandma about struggling with finding a friend. Maybe like me, she hadn't wanted to worry anyone with her sadness and loneliness, and had kept all her true feelings in her heart.

That Friday after school, I wanted to sing with joy that I was finally free, but I couldn't. It seemed the music had died inside me.

When I arrived at the house, Papi and the boys didn't even notice my presence. They were playing basketball with the neighbors across the street. I wanted to go to them, but like always, Ashley Jane and her friends had beat me to it. I wanted nothing to do with them. Besides, I had never played basketball before, and I didn't want them laughing at me when I inevitably messed up on my first try.

I heard Mami's and Mrs. Boden's laughter coming from inside our house, and resentment hardened my heart. It wasn't fair for me to be angry that they were becoming good friends, but I couldn't help feeling confused.

I lifted my eyes to the sky, but it was still too light for the stars to come out, much less for one to fall so I could make a wish. Mine didn't come true anymore though. My friend Estrellita hadn't found her way to me.

Something had broken in the move. I had broken. Usually, a song would be at the tip of my tongue. Now there was silence.

Since Mrs. Boden was inside my house, I couldn't go in yet. The only place I could think to go was the backyard, where there was an abandoned shed.

Montserrat had warned us that the Jensens didn't want anyone in there.

I didn't care. There wasn't any other place to hide.

The door wasn't even locked. It opened with a creak. The place smelled musty, like it hadn't been opened in decades. Dust danced on a sunbeam coming through the dirty glass of the window. I stepped in and closed the door behind me.

Boxes were piled by the walls and on top of them . . .

A head.

"Ahhhh!" I screamed, and covered my face.

Outside, my brothers and their friends kept laughing. No one had heard me. Slowly, I put my hands down and opened my eyes.

The stuffed head of a majestic deer, with antlers like tree branches, was mounted on the wall. Its beady black eyes unseeing and unmoving.

This gorgeous animal had died in its prime only to end up mounted on the wall of a shed no one ever went in.

I had promised Lela I'd be brave and strong. But I was too tired. I started crying.

No one but a poor stuffed deer was there to see my sadness. Although the place was filthy, I slid down to the floor, and I stayed there for a long time. But eventually, my tears ran out.

"Ay, María Emilia," I said aloud. "At least you're not that deer." I chuckled at myself.

A whining sound startled me. And when I lifted my head, I came face-to-face with the little tan dog.

CHAPTER 15

The dog had the exact same coloring as Estrellita. The tan body faded out to black along the dog's flattened snout and perked ears. From up close, it looked more like a French bull dog, but not purebred.

Kneeling, I put my hand out and waited. I wished Mami could see that I was patient after all.

I was rewarded when, after a bit of snuffling, the dog took a tentative step in my direction. I held my breath so I wouldn't spook her away. When she finally made it all the way to me, I noticed she didn't have a collar or tags. Though she looked taken care of, she had to be a stray. I scratched her chin gently, and she looked up at me with large brown eyes, soft and velvety with trust. Then she blinked.

She had an expression like she was smiling.

Somehow it was exactly the way Estrellita always looked at me.

"Hola, Estrellita," I said.

She licked my face to her heart's content, and when she was done, she snuggled into my lap. The song that had hid in the knot pressing against my chest finally unraveled.

> *The mountain is hard to climb*
> *When you think you're all alone.*
> *In the darkness, the wind blowing,*
> *The doubts are louder,*
> *The fear is stronger.*
> *Just extend your hand and you'll find*
> *Those you love are never far.*
> *Across oceans, mountains, rivers,*
> *Years or worlds apart,*
> *In spite of death,*
> *Love knows no end.*
> *The bonds can stretch,*
> *But they won't break unless you forget*
> *That those you love are never far.*

After the rain,

The rainbow is always there

To remind you that those you love are never far.

Brighter days are on the way

And the tears of yesterday, like the rain,

Cleansed the path you walk today.

I sang the words over and over, and the dog closed her eyes. Soon, she was snoring, as if she'd been walking for a long time, and now she could finally rest. The sound of her breathing helped me relax too.

I watched the dog dreaming, her legs twitching, her whiskers trembling. What was she dreaming about? I covered my mouth so my laughter wouldn't wake her. But soon, I realized that I was going to be pinned under a dreaming puppy for a long time. Old habits are hard to break, and even though it was Friday, I had a ton of homework to start because I was behind in every class. I dragged my backpack over to me. When he found out we only had one laptop at home for the whole family to share, Mr. Taylor, my new math teacher, let me bring a school tablet home so I could catch up.

Ten finished math worksheets and a whole rendition of the songs from the seventh-grade graduation later, I realized the dog was awake. Again, her eyes reminded me of how Estrellita used to look at me when she sensed I carried too many troubles in my heart. There was so much love in the dog's gaze, the words tumbled out of me one right after the other.

She listened without judgment, and when I was done confessing I wasn't the daughter my parents expected me to be, she shook her head, as if telling me to stop calling myself bad names.

"Okay," I said.

The dog blinked a few times and yawned.

"Are you still tired?" I asked in Spanish. I wondered if I should be speaking English to her, but one thing was true all over the world: Pets speak the language of love and kindness. Besides, *I* was too tired to speak one more word in English.

But instead of snuggling against me again, she jumped to her feet and started sniffing my backpack.

"What do you want, baby?" I asked, my heart blooming with tenderness at her twinkling eyes, the twitch of her ears, and the happy wag of her tail.

She looked up at me and barked once.

"You're hungry!" I said, thrilled that even if English gave me a hard time, at least I was a fast learner of Doggish.

I looked around me, but there was nothing in this shed for her to eat. The dog kept sniffing at my backpack as if she were trying to find a treasure.

"You know? I might have something in there," I said.

I rummaged in the backpack and found a chocolate, which was out of the question for the dog, and a sandwich from lunch. I unwrapped it and placed it on the floor. With her nose, she moved the mystery meat aside and started eating the cheese. I'd never seen such bright orange cheese in my life, and I didn't like it. The puppy seemed to love it though.

Like my Estrellita.

"Estrellita," I said, petting her head while she ate.

She looked up at me again and smiled.

"Mimilia!" Francisco's tiny voice called from outside the shed, and I jumped.

Through the little, grime-covered window I could see it was almost dark outside. It must have been close to ten.

I couldn't leave Estrellita out by herself. If it were a little earlier, I know my family would've helped me figure out if she had a home, but being so late, that was out of the question.

"Mimilia!" Now my two brothers called for me. The worry in Mateo's voice clawed up my spine and made me shiver.

"Come here, Estrellita," I said, hoping she'd follow me to my house instead of bolting out to the darkness. But I shouldn't have worried. Estrellita stayed close to me as I made my way toward my brothers.

"You were in there the whole time?" Mateo asked, pointing at the shed as if it were a dungeon.

"Maybe, maybe not," I teased him.

"What were you doing there?" Francisco asked, taking my backpack from me. But it was heavier than he expected. Before he dropped it, I caught the shoulder strap.

"It's okay, baby. I got it," I said. "I was doing homework, and look who I found . . ."

"A ghost?" Mateo asked, his voice quivering. I knew he was mostly being silly but was also a little scared.

Estrellita chose that moment to jump out of the shadows.

Mateo screamed, "A wolf!"

Francisco added, "A giant rat! It's stinky!"

Estrellita ran circles around them, and when my brothers realized it was a dog, their eyes lit up like suns.

"A dog!" they said at the same time.

Mateo knelt down to pet her, and she licked his face like she'd known him all her life. He looked at me and said in an awed voice, "She looks like Estrellita."

"Let me see!" Francisco said, shoving Mateo aside.

Mateo wouldn't budge, and soon they were wrestling each other. The dog once again started running in circles around them, barking.

"What's this escándalo?" Papi asked, coming out of the house. "Shhh. The neighbors are sleeping!"

The three of us and even the dog went quiet. Francisco pointed at the dog, while Mateo tried not to laugh.

"Who's this?" Papi asked. He too knelt to pet Estrellita, who'd flopped on her back for him to rub her belly. She was a smart dog.

"I was doing homework—"

"Sulking, you mean," Francisco said with an annoying smile.

How did he even know what *sulking* was?

"Was not!" I replied. "I was . . . singing, and she came out from behind some crates."

"Was she there the whole time?" Papi asked, sounding worried.

I shook my head. "She wasn't there when I went in. She must have snuck in behind me when I was . . . looking at something else."

Papi pressed his lips. "Remember Montserrat said not to go in there?"

"But we live here, Papi. Besides, all the Jensens have in there is boxes and a stuffed deer mounted on the wall."

"Stuffed deer?" asked Mateo. "I want to see it."

My dad gave him a warning look.

"Believe me," I said, "it's not the kind of stuffed animal you're thinking about."

Papi sighed, and I said, "But, Papi, don't you see? She looks like—"

"Estrellita," Mami said. She was standing in the doorway. Who knew how long she'd been there watching us with the dog? She had a dreamy expression I didn't know how to read.

"Mami . . ." I said, but I couldn't say anything else. I stared into her eyes, hoping she'd put into words all the feelings that were crashing inside me, and that I couldn't translate into any language.

Mami nodded, and Mateo, obviously fluent in Mami's every expression and gesture, cheered.

Mami put a hand up and said, "She seems well taken care of. I'm sure she has a family."

"But she doesn't have a collar or tags," I said.

"We can go looking for her family," Francisco said. "I have a flashlight." For effect, he clicked the flashlight on and off, blinding us all in the process.

"We don't know if we can keep a dog in the rental," Papi said.

There was a heavy silence, but when I looked up, I saw Mami and Papi having one of those silent conversations in the language Lela said only parents understood.

A knot grew in my throat when I thought of Estrellita staying out all night, but then Mami said, "It's late. I say we go to bed."

"And the dog?" Francisco asked in his tiny voice that belonged in a cartoon.

Mami shrugged. "Bring her in, of course."

"Yay," my brothers and I cheered, jumping in place. Estrellita joined the celebration by howling.

The Bodens' front porch light came on, and we all giggled silently, even Mami and Papi.

"Let's go inside, Estrellita," I said.

"We'll make her a bed in our room!" Mateo said, running inside the house.

I looked at my mom, and she put a stop to my brothers right away. "Now, Mati, give Mimilia the chance to have a sleepover with a friend."

Mateo and Francisco had eaten with the Bodens earlier, and they grumbled when Mami sent them to bed but still obeyed. My parents and I ate a quick dinner in the quiet kitchen. Once I'd helped clean up, Estrellita clambered up the stairs behind me to the attic room that still held the heat of the day.

"Let's make a bed for her right here on the floor," Mami said, folding some blankets.

But Estrellita jumped on my bed, circled once, twice, three times, until she finally seemed satisfied enough to curl up in a crescent and go right to sleep.

She was snoring before my mom could protest.

Mami and I laughed quietly. Mami caressed my hair and said, "It's nice to see you smiling again . . . I know this hasn't been fun for you . . ."

That this whole experience hadn't been fun was an understatement. It had been horrible!

But my parents had tried to do what was best for our family.

"It's okay, Mami," I said. "The hard things are worth it in the end, right?"

"Right," she said, hugging me close to her. "Go to sleep now. Tomorrow we'll make posters to find her family."

Mami went downstairs, humming softly.

In spite of what she said, in my heart, I believed my wish had finally been granted. My cat had found a way back to my side.

Estrellita had arrived to stay with me forever, and I was never going to let her go.

CHAPTER 16

The scent of something delicious baking woke me up.

"Papi is making croissants!" Mateo yelled from downstairs a second after I opened my eyes.

Next to me was the warmth of a dog.

She hadn't been a dream, then!

For the first time since the move, I wasn't dreading the day ahead.

Estrellita jumped from the bed and barked at me to hurry up before all the croissants were taken.

If I closed my eyes, it was almost like we were back home. Our real home, with Lela singing to her plants while Papi baked a weekend tradition.

I dashed downstairs after my new pet. But even before I reached the kitchen, the scent turned bitter.

On the counter was a cookie sheet with the smallest, ugliest croissants I'd seen in my life. They looked like charred shrimp.

Mateo and Francisco eyed them with repulsion.

Papi stared at the croissants like he couldn't believe his eyes.

I couldn't help it. I started laughing.

Soon, we were all laughing.

"What is that?" I asked when I could speak.

Papi shrugged. "I got up at the crack of dawn to surprise Mami before she headed to the office. But I think I made a mistake measuring the powdered yeast. It didn't work . . ."

"Imperial system," I said, shaking my head.

"That could be it," Papi said, wagging his index finger like I'd discovered the fault in the plan. "It's hard to get used to the different measures, the altitude, the different water . . . The list of variables is endless!"

Mateo flopped to the floor, staring at the ceiling like he'd never recover from the disappointment. "Any time now, Mami will be done getting ready. It would've been nice to send her off with a happy surprise."

"She's going to the office on a Saturday?" I asked with dismay.

"You know her . . ." Papi said, shaking his head. "She wanted to get ahead of her week, planning a few things for her students. There's a girl from Puerto Rico who can sure use the extra help."

An unwelcome thought intruded: Why did she spend so much time on her students? What about us here at home?

"We can make her toast," Francisco said. Papi looked disappointed.

And then I remembered the food Montserrat had brought for us on the day we'd arrived. I ran to the fridge and grabbed a tube that read *Giant Croissants*.

"What about these?" The list of ingredients was longer than the things I missed from home, and there were some words that seemed more like letter soup than ingredients. But it said *cinnamon croissants* right there on the label.

Papi shrugged. "Why not?"

He pulled on a tab until the top of the tube came off in a satisfying pop.

"Oooh," my brothers and I said with a sigh, looking at how he unrolled the cardboard and placed a sheet of dough on the floured countertop.

Estrellita jumped as if she were trying to see what we were so interested in, and Mateo picked her up so she could see.

"What's that?" I asked, tracing dots premade on the dough.

"*This* is magic," Papi said with awe in his voice.

He went on to separate the dough on the dotted line into triangles. Then he rolled one and placed it on the cookie sheet. After Mateo put Estrellita down and washed his hands, he, Francisco, and I helped Papi with the rest.

The croissants looked tiny and sad. Like the pale twins of the charred shrimp.

"Have faith," Papi said.

Estrellita barked and lowered her face as if she were giving a tiny prayer, and we all laughed.

Papi put the cookie sheet in the oven. My brothers cleaned the counter, and I went behind them, sweeping the floor. Estrellita licked the crumbs I'd missed.

"Great teamwork!" Papi exclaimed.

The smell of cinnamon and sugar permeated the kitchen, overpowering that of the burned croissants that had never risen.

By the time Mami came out of the bathroom, guided by a smiling Estrellita, the croissants were beautifully arranged on a plate next to the coffee my dad had prepared for her.

Mami's smile was contagious. "What's this?"

"That is magic, Mamá," Francisco said. "Try it."

She bit into a croissant. Papi and I exchanged a nervous look.

Mami closed her eyes and sighed. "This is the best thing I've had in a long time!"

My brothers cheered. Estrellita barked in approval.

Mami finished her coffee, and after a kiss, she said, "I'll be back a little after one. Have fun!"

And she walked out, leaving behind the scent of her jasmine perfume and the promise of an afternoon together.

Even with Mami gone, Saturdays were chore days. Papi wouldn't budge. So many things had changed in our life, but apparently chores were one of those sacred traditions that persisted through life-changing events.

The boys helped Papi clean the bathrooms. My job was putting laundry away. In Argentina, Violeta and I had hung laundry on a clothesline. Here in the house we had a dryer. Although now the washing was a million times easier, the putting away was still the worst. Estrellita's "help" as she snuffled through the clothes made it take even longer, but I was so happy to have her with me. I took a picture of my dog sitting inside a basket, covered with towels.

Once we were finally done, the boys ran out to play with the Bodens, and I sat at the computer to share the picture with Violeta. I was immediately surprised.

On her social media, Violeta had tagged me in a picture of our class on their pre-graduation trip to Córdoba with a sign that said *We miss you, María Emilia!*

My eyes burned with tears but not only the sad kind. I was happy for them. We'd planned on the trip forever, and although I couldn't be there with them, they'd thought of me like I thought about them all the time.

I replied with heart emojis and sent her the picture of Estrellita, hashtagged *LaundryDog*. I wished I could travel home as easily as a message online and see her reaction in person.

I headed toward the shed to deal with my mixed feelings.

"Are you sure you're going to be okay in that shed, Mimilia?" Papi asked. "It must be scorching in there."

"I like it," I said, shrugging. "Come on, girl."

Estrellita followed me. The air was suffocating for September.

I wondered when my body would understand this change of season.

The whole morning went in the blink of an eye as I thought about my friends and did the rest of my homework, singing my favorite songs from movies and the radio for Estrellita. It felt like the bands had been broken around my heart, and finally the music poured out of me.

When I had warmed up enough, I started singing my own song, "Those You Love Are Never Far." The melody had been born in my heart.

The whole time I tried variations in pitch and tempo, and Estrellita watched me with attention, her head bobbing at the rhythm of my voice.

I wasn't good at writing letters like Celestina had been, but maybe one day a kid missing home and feeling out of place would listen to my song and feel like someone else in another place and time understood them. Maybe they'd feel less alone. The thought kept me going for hours.

It wasn't until my stomach growled that I noticed what time it was.

"Ready for some lunch?" Mami asked behind me, startling me.

"Mami!" I said, and ran to hug her.

She looked tired, her eyes a little puffy, but she still smiled. "I love to hear you singing again."

"I've been writing," I said.

Her eyes lit up. "Really? Will you sing it to me?"

I cringed. "I will when it's finished. I promise."

There was something about sharing my work before it was done that blocked me from actually finishing it.

"I get it," Mami said. "Back when I wrote, if I shared the idea with someone, it was like my brain was satisfied that it already had an audience. Then I lost steam."

"Exactly," I said.

My stomach growled, and Mami laughed. "But I don't want you here all day. Why don't you see if Ashley Jane wants to . . . hang out?"

"Maybe later," I said, with zero intention of even looking at Ashley Jane.

"How about a sandwich, then?"

"Sure! Estrellita's hungry too."

Mami looked at the dog, whose tongue was lolling out. "I'm sure we can find something that's okay for her to eat."

"After lunch, can you help me make the signs to see if she has a home?" The words cost me a lot to say aloud.

"Sure," she said.

When we went in, the house was eerily quiet.

"Where are the boys and Papi?"

Mami was taking out cheese and salami from the fridge. "The Bodens invited them to a fútbol game."

"To watch?"

"Actually, the fall league is about to start, and they needed players," she said.

"I'm glad the boys are finding friends so quickly."

She must have heard the longing in my voice because she said, "And I'm glad you found a furry friend to keep you company until your human friends come along . . ."

"Maybe they never will."

Now that I'd put into words my greatest fear, my heart started pounding.

Mami shook her head. "I assure you, Emilia, you'll find your people before you know it."

I hugged her. "I already have my people. You, Papi, and the boys. They're annoying, but they're cute, so I think we can keep them."

Mami laughed. "And if we make the posters, and no one claims her, we can keep this puppy too."

When we finished lunch and handwriting posters, Mami drove Estrellita and me around the neighborhood to pin the signs on bulletin boards and posts. We left one at the vet, who said she'd seen the puppy around the neighborhood, but that she didn't know who the owners were.

Then we went to the ice-cream shop where the older teenagers liked to hang out. The man at the gas station next to it said he'd also seen Estrellita, that she kept him company during his night shift, but he had never met her owners. Maybe she was a stray after all.

When we went back home, the boys and Papi hadn't arrived yet. Mami wanted to take a nap, and I, happy that no one had claimed my dog, headed to my room with Estrellita. I wanted to read one of Celestina's letters.

I browsed until I found one I could certainly relate to.

Dear Nonna Rosa,

The heat in this place is unbearable. The humidity is suffocating. Mama says it's the humidity that allows for such vibrant green. But between you and me, I could do with a duller shade of green in exchange for some relief. The mosquitoes have feasted on me for weeks. After so many stings, my skin doesn't swell up anymore. So that's the silver lining I promised I'd include in every letter. Happy now?

I'm sorry I'm a little snappy. Sometimes it's easier to let the negative emotions run their course until they dissolve like dew in the mornings. Did I ever tell you how beautiful the roses look in the morning when I go feed the chickens? The pinks, reds, and whites seem to glow with millions of tiny drops on each delicate petal. The other day I saw my first hummingbird. Have I ever told you about them?

They're the smallest birds you could imagine.

A cross between a butterfly, a bumblebee, and a sparrow, with a thin, long beak to drink the nectar out of the flowers. Iridescent green feathers cover its body, but they look like tiny scales. I've never seen anything so beautiful in my life, Nonna. I wish I knew how to draw to send you a likeness because words fail me. They're magical, and apparently, they only live in America, which makes this move worth it when everything seems so hard.

Seeing one hovering over the flowers made me happy on a day that my heart was heavy with longing for your voice and love, and the company of at least one friend. Nafiza, the girl from the ship, continued her journey to Entre Ríos with her family. She promised to write, but you know the price of a stamp. Finding friends at my age isn't easy! But at least I have Mamma, Babbo, and the boys to keep me company. I don't know what I'd do without them.

So there. See? I let all the negative feelings run their course, and the memory of the hummingbird broke free like sunshine through storm clouds to help me see that I have the most important thing of all: my family.

Oh! And books, Nonna! The teacher comes around once a month with a collection of books we can borrow. I might not be able to attend school since we live so far, but at least we have books! She let me borrow a tome of <u>Grimms' Fairy Tales</u>.

I'll tell you more about my favorite ones in the next letter. Mamma is going to the post office soon, and besides, I ran out of paper.

I miss you and I love you.

Celestina

My poor great-grandma. So she *did* spend time longing for a friend. At least I had a dog. I gently pried one of Mateo's stuffed animals from Estrellita's happy mouth. I needed to get this puppy a chew toy.

She jumped beside me on the bed while I hummed the song that wanted to break free from my heart. But I was afraid to let it go because I knew once it did, it would bring along feelings I wasn't ready to deal with yet.

"Guess how many goals I scored?" Francisco exclaimed, barging into my room.

Estrellita was immediately electric with excitement.

Mateo ran in after Francisco, and they both spoke at the same time.

I couldn't tell what they were saying, but their little eyes were shining like sparks.

"One at a time!" I bellowed.

They both quit speaking at once.

I pointed at Mateo. "Tell me first."

He took a deep breath and said, "We made it on the team!"

"I scored three goals," Francisco said.

"And I saved four!" Mateo added.

In bits and pieces I gathered that their first official fútbol game had been an absolute success.

"They said I'm just like Messi," Francisco said.

"And that I'm the best goalie they've ever had," Mateo added, his chest puffed up with pride.

I caught Papi's eyes, and I quickly looked away so I wouldn't laugh. I didn't want to hurt my brothers' feelings.

They were proud of themselves in a way I'd never seen before.

"Now we're gonna practice with the Bodens," Francisco

said. Then he turned toward Mateo and said in perfect English, "Let's go, bro!"

That had me laughing for a long time.

They left in a flurry of movement and color, like iridescent hummingbirds. It was time to walk Estrellita anyway, so I left the room to take her out.

When I walked into the kitchen, the phone rang, and my heart jumped to my throat.

What if it was Estrellita's owners wanting to take her back?

Quickly, I scurried out of the kitchen before anyone answered the call.

CHAPTER 17

On Wednesday night, when once again my dad and my brothers headed to a soccer practice, my dog and I went back to the shed so I could sing in peace.

I was belting out a version of my song, when Estrellita's ears perked up and she jumped to her feet.

"What is it?" I asked.

Someone knocked on the shed's door.

My senses kicked into hyperalertness. If it had been my mom coming to get me for dinner, she'd have just walked in.

I waited in silence, and Estrellita whined.

"Cookie? Are you there?" a boy asked from the other side of the door.

Estrellita started scratching the door frantically.

"Hello?" I said, slowly opening the door and peeking outside.

But Estrellita snuck between my legs and darted out.

She jumped on the boy. She was tiny, but somehow the boy was on the ground.

"Estrellita, stop!" I said, afraid she was attacking him, but then I realized she was kissing him.

"Hey! There you are!" the boy said.

He was sprawled on the ground, dry leaves sticking to his hair. Estrellita stood on his chest, barking. He laughed like he'd seen the most wonderful thing in the world, then rolled to the side to stand up face-to-face with me.

"You stole my dog!" Donovan said in Spanish.

"I didn't steal your dog!" I replied in English, the words coming out with such force he seemed stunned into silence.

I gathered Estrellita up into my arms so he couldn't take her away. She couldn't be his puppy. There had to be a mistake. She was affectionate and friendly. That was all.

As if she could read my thoughts, she started licking my face, and the thought of her having licked Donovan's made me flinch.

A cloud passed over Donovan's eyes when he saw Estrellita snuggling up to me.

"If you didn't steal her, why is Cookie here?"

"Cookie?" I spat back. "You're confused. This is Estrellita." I knew I was being unreasonable, but I couldn't stop myself.

Donovan took a deep breath as if he were arming himself with patience. "I know my dog, and she knows me too."

My blood froze in my veins. "Why would you name her Cookie?"

"Because she looks like a snickerdoodle. But *Snickerdoodle* was too long for such a tiny dog."

"Cookie," I muttered. Wasn't it obvious that she was an Estrella, her eyes sparkling like stars?

She licked my face again as if telling me everything was going to be all right.

Donovan showed me the crumpled poster in his hand. "I found this on Main Street over the weekend, but I didn't have the chance to stop by until today."

I had never regretted doing the right thing more than now.

"How did you lose her?" I asked.

Donovan sighed. "I didn't lose her. She ran away. She likes

music. A car full of teenagers drove past my street, and she followed them. When she realized I was chasing her, she thought we were playing tag, and she kept running."

"She does like to be chased," I said, thinking of my brothers running circles around the yard with her until the three of them got dizzy and collapsed.

"I've been looking for days. Julián left for college last weekend. He asked me to watch her for him, and I failed him."

I was silent, taking in how much he seemed to care about his brother.

Donovan's eyes were brimming with tears. "It's the only thing he ever asked of me, and I couldn't even do that, you know? After looking at the shelter, and everywhere else I thought she could be, I saw a shooting star and made a wish. When I went into the gas station to ask if they'd seen her, I saw the poster. It was literally a sign from the universe."

He looked around and his eyes stopped at the stuffed deer on the wall. "This place is—"

"Weird?"

Donovan laughed.

I realized we'd been speaking Spanish and English—Spanglish—the whole time.

"Weird like my Argentine accent that doesn't match your expectations from TV shows?"

He bit his lip and shrugged. "Wow. You do know how to keep a grudge."

"No, I don't!" I protested, vowing never to forgive him for this. When I realized what I was thinking, I fidgeted.

"I'm so sorry about that day, okay?" he said. "I didn't know. I've only ever met Argentines from Buenos Aires or Rosario, and they have the same accent."

I was offended on Papi's behalf. "No, they don't!"

Donovan looked at me with disbelief. "Of course they do!"

"And how do you know? You've met a few random Argentines, and all of a sudden, you're an expert? My dad is from Rosario, and I tell you, he speaks nothing like a porteño."

Estrellita seemed to be listening to us, gazing at Donovan and me like she didn't really know what to do, who to comfort first. But couldn't she see I needed her the most?

Maybe it would've been better if I'd never—

I brushed away the thought before it was fully formed.

If it hadn't been for Estrellita, life would've been too hard.

The sun was going down. How would I face another day without even Estrellita's company to give me strength?

Estrellita whined as if she knew what I was feeling.

"She's good at comforting people."

Donovan scratched behind her ear. "You know? She was meant to become an emotional support dog, but she never passed the test."

"An emotional support dog?"

I'd seen working dogs around with their cute official-looking vests. The one who'd sat next to Francisco on the airplane had worn a red one.

"How come she didn't pass the test?" I asked, ready to fight the world for her.

Donovan smiled as if the story was the funniest thing in the world. "She's smart. But she's too hyper to sit still for a long time. She never did what the trainers expected her to do, but she always went above and beyond. In her own way, you know. Like I told you she heard music and ran after the kids. Maybe she thought they needed help."

Estrellita had heard me crying and had come to comfort me . . .

"She likes it when I sing to her."

He rubbed his neck. "She has great taste in music." He winced although I was the one blushing. "Everything seemed to stop to hear your voice. You sounded magical."

Emotion overwhelmed me, but for the first time since I'd been here in Red Ledges, it wasn't sadness or loneliness.

"At least my voice survived the trip here . . ."

"What do you mean?"

"I feel like I lost a bunch of things on our plane ride," I said, surprising myself. "Not just my luggage. I seem to have lost my ability to speak English. I was the best one in my class back home. School used to be my favorite, but now I hate it. My cat, Estrellita, died the day we left . . ."

Estrellita's ear went up like an antenna detecting a crisis. She licked my hand and wriggled until I put her down. She dashed straight out of the shed.

"Cookie, no!" Donovan yelled, but he wasn't quick enough to stop her.

I ran after him.

Cookie/Estrellita hadn't gone far. She was running in circles around Mateo, who'd left the car door open.

My brother rubbed his eyes as if he were still sleepy. "Estrellita, I'm too tired to chase you. Give me a break."

He threw himself on the lawn. His face was red and sweaty.

"Mati, are you okay? How did your game go?"

My little brother looked at me with surprise, as if I'd just materialized. "Oh! I didn't see you, Mimilia."

"Mimilia?" Donovan asked.

I sent him a *don't you dare* look, and he had the good sense to clasp his lips shut.

Mateo's white uniform was completely smeared in reddish mud.

"Are you okay?" I asked, brushing my brother's hair from his face.

He sighed. "I guess, but . . . what's an alien number?"

"Alien number?"

He sat up, propping himself with an elbow. "Yes, at the game, when the ref was checking our roster, John-William asked me if my alien number was legal. Everyone laughed. Even his dad, but a mom shushed them. And I think it's something bad. Are we *aliens*? I thought Utah was on planet Earth . . ."

He looked so worried, like everything he'd believed about himself teetered on my reply, that I didn't have the heart to laugh at him.

"If you're anything other than human, then that's because you're an angel. Don't worry about it, okay?" But I still wondered how our six-year-old neighbor knew what an alien number was, and why his father had laughed instead of correcting him.

Apparently Mateo had already moved on from the problem because he grinned and said in English, "I don't know if I'm an angel. But I played like a pro today. It was amazing."

"You did?" Donovan asked.

Mateo puffed up his cheeks, and in a failed attempt at being humble, he said, "I slid-tackled this kid? He was like a giant next to me, Mimilia. I took the ball away from him . . . But I broke my tail when I fell."

"You broke your tail?"

He rubbed his backside, and I understood.

"Oh! Your bum you mean!"

Mateo flashed me a grateful toothless smile. "Yes, that. My cola."

He clambered back to his feet and walked into the house, where Papi and Francisco were resting on the cool floor.

Donovan and I looked at each other and broke into laughter.

"He. Broke. His. Tail!" he said between hiccups, clutching his stomach.

I couldn't catch my breath. The tears of sadness and loneliness I'd been containing for so long broke free and mixed with the sublime joy of how my brother had translated literally. But then, when he was corrected, he hadn't reacted badly at all.

I wanted to be unselfconscious like him. When had other people's opinions started dictating how I felt and how I reacted?

"Your brother is awesome," Donovan said.

"Wait until you meet Francisco."

As if she agreed, Estrellita barked and ran around Donovan and me. I knew I should call her Cookie, but the habit would be hard to break.

There was a charged silence between Donovan and me. The time had come for him to go, taking my dog.

"In case you don't know," I said, "she likes cheese snacks. Let me give you the ones we got her yesterday."

Donavan hesitated, but I could see the warring emotions on his face.

"Wait," he finally said. "I have an idea."

My heart jolted, and I tried not to jump to any conclusions. I didn't want to be disappointed. But his next words caught me off guard all the same.

"Tirzah, Beto, and I have a rock band."

"A what?"

He pointed at his black T-shirt. It had a logo that said *Maná*.

Maná is one of the most popular bands in the Spanish-language music world. They'd been around when my parents were teenagers, and although I didn't usually love the old stuff my parents listened to, some Maná songs were timeless.

"You're part of Maná?"

Donovan grinned again. "Not Maná. Los Galácticos."

"I thought Los Galácticos was a fútbol team."

Donovan shook his head. "Yes, the Real Madrid, but that's not why we chose that name."

A car drove down my street and stopped by the Bodens'. Ashley Jane and her friends got out, sounding like a flock of parrots, wearing their little volleyball uniforms.

Donovan's face hardened at the sight of those kids.

"In any case, we have a band," he said. "And my dog happens to be our mascot. How come you didn't recognize her from our logo?"

He showed me the back of his phone. He had the same sticker that he, Beto, and Tirzah had placed on their school T-shirts on the first day of school. Now that I could really look at it, I recognized Estrellita—Cookie—immediately.

"Seeing this logo, I insist: Estrellita fits her better," I said. "She's an astronaut dog!"

He sighed, but my shoulders sagged. It was his dog after all.

To avoid the inevitable, I turned the conversation back to the band. "What do you play?"

He shrugged. "Covers of popular songs from the radio. From the nineties all the way to modern times. I'm the guitarist. Tirzah plays the drums, and Beto is on keyboard and synthesizer."

"Who sings?"

"That *was* Lucas Anderson. But his family moved to Salt Lake at the end of June."

"Salt Lake's not that far," I said. Although the four hours from the Salt Lake airport to Red Ledges had seemed eternal.

Donovan's mouth twitched. "It's not *if* you can drive yourself around. His parents promised they'd come visit every other weekend, but Lucas only came down for a fútbol tournament and we didn't even have time to practice once. I tried singing, but the truth is, my voice isn't very reliable at the moment." Right on cue, his voice squeaked.

"You need a singer?" I asked, to make sure I understood what he was saying.

"Yes, we need a singer," Donovan said. "And have I told you how awesome your voice is? It's like nothing I've ever heard before."

My cheeks burned with the unexpected compliment. I'd sung all my life. Even before I knew how to speak, I'd sing to myself in my crib in the mornings before my parents picked me up.

"I thought it was the radio when I first heard you," he said.

"Now you're exaggerating, Donovan."

He laughed.

"Red Ledges' Battle of the Bands competition is coming up

soon. It's at the end of the term right before the holidays. We've been signed up since last year. We worked for months to get the fee to get in, and finally my brother chipped in the rest before he left for college. In any case, no matter how much we paid for it or when the competition is, we don't have a singer. I'd love to have you be part of the band."

"Don't you have to talk to your friends first?"

"Of course," he said. "But once they hear your voice? They're gonna be thrilled to have you."

I looked down at the ground. The leaves crunched under my feet when I shifted. I didn't know what to say.

When I didn't reply, Donovan added, "It counts as one of the school clubs."

I bit my lip as I considered, and he added, "We practice at my house every night at seven. You could come and see Cookie, or Estrellita, or whatever you want to call her. It's a win-win, see?"

I wasn't convinced. "What's the Battle of the Bands exactly?"

I only knew the term from the shirt that Ashley Jane— well, her mom—had given me.

The girls across the street were still on their front lawn. Kel had started singing about someone sitting in a tree. I didn't understand the rest of the lyrics, but Donovan was blushing bright red.

"Let's go inside the shed and you can tell me more about it," I said.

Donovan followed me, and in the meantime, he explained, "The Battle of the Bands is a competition that takes place right before winter break. It's part of the Bring on the Light celebration for the winter holidays. There are plays, a winter craft market, and a silent auction. When my brother was in school, he and his friends, the first Galácticos, entered the battle to win stuff for different projects they really cared about. One year it was the veteran museum. There was no recognition of our Hispanic, Black, and Native American veterans, so Los Galácticos earned money to include a display in their honor. Then it was the animal shelter and the kitten and puppy rescue society. That's where Julián found Cookie."

"What is it going to be for this year?" I asked.

Donovan shrugged. "We haven't come up with something we all agreed on yet. With Lucas gone . . . I don't know. I was starting to lose enthusiasm for the whole thing. But if you joined the band, our project could be modernizing the book mobile collection."

"What's a book mobile?" I asked, pacing the shed, ideas buzzing in my mind.

"It's an old van that goes from town to town with free books for people."

Like the book cart that stopped in Celestina's town when she was little! "I didn't know those existed."

Donovan nodded. "They go to mobile home parks, camping spots, and RV parks . . . All the books are super old though. Some are classics, but you know some classics can contain all this outdated language, super-harmful stuff. There's nothing a kid our age would fall in love with. I mean, Tom Sawyer might have been fun and exciting fifty years ago, but can you imagine Mateo reading it?"

"Never," I said. "He'd run back to his game on Mami's phone."

"Exactly. There are so many amazing things out there, but we're still reading things from two centuries ago. No offense, but when was the last time you read something about a beautiful girl who had to leave her homeland and start from scratch in a new place?"

Had he called me beautiful? My cheeks burned. Was this the same boy who'd made fun of my accent not too long ago?

His excitement was catching like a wave of light and energy that turned everything brighter. Up until now, I'd felt like a little piece of driftwood bobbing over giant ocean waves. Here was an option to grab ahold of a buoy.

There had to be a reason why I was here in this moment in this period of my life. We'd moved because of my mom's work, and my parents' dream of a better future for our family, but there had to be a reason for *me* to be here. For me to have all these talents and all this time to use them to help someone else. Maybe in the meantime, I'd be helping myself too.

Donovan must have seen that I was leaning toward accepting.

He pointed at Estrellita, who was back and dozing at my feet, and said, "I mean, even if we don't win, you can, you know, hang with Tirzah, Beto, and me. And you can see my dog. We can even call her Estrellita—when you're around."

What would Celestina do?

Celestina would jump at the adventure.

"I'm in," I said.

Donovan stretched his hand out to me, and we shook. "Deal."

CHAPTER 18

The first thing I did the next day at school was look for Los Galácticos. I found them in the music room.

Beto was playing the piano, a melody so upbeat and happy, my mood spiked instantly. I knew this song. Tirzah clapped the beat with her hands, and Donovan played an invisible air guitar.

This song needed a voice. Could I find mine?

My heart was beating so hard. What if I started singing and ruined the moment?

But I couldn't hold it in anymore. I took a big breath and let the song free.

Beto's fingers stumbled on the piano, and my voice hitched like a question mark. But when he saw it was me at the door, his eyes widened, and he continued playing.

Tirzah smiled radiantly at me. When I reached the chorus, she joined an octave lower. Our voices matched smoothly. I had yet to cross the threshold, but Donovan waved me in from his spot next to the piano. Once I was side by side with them, Donovan joined Tirzah in the chorus. The harmony of our three voices was perfect.

It made a part of my heart vibrate in a way that tore down the awkwardness from the first day I'd met them.

Until the bell rang, implacable.

My song died on my lips, although my heart still beat with its rhythm.

Beto played the last measure, and when the final note resonated in the air with an echo, he looked at me and said in Spanish, "*That* was amazing!"

That's all it took for the euphoria to bubble.

"Who could guess this shy girl had such a big voice?"

"And that accent?" Donovan teased me. "It was perfect."

I wasn't shy, and my accent hadn't been perfect. My *r* had over-rolled when I'd sung the word *friends*, and my cheeks were still burning over it, but they all pretended they hadn't heard it, or maybe they weren't pretending. Maybe I was just being hard on myself.

"Gracias," I said.

"I guess this means you're in?" Donovan asked.

I nodded.

"Yes!" cheered Tirzah and Beto.

Soon, ninth graders were starting to arrive for first period, and a tall boy sent us an annoyed look.

"I need to head to EL," I said, grabbing my stuff.

"And I have Gov and Civ," Beto said.

Donovan rolled his eyes. "Who has time for Gov and Civ when we finally have a singer?"

But there was no choice but to head to class anyway.

Unlike the previous days though, now I knew I wasn't alone. My new friends saw what I could do with my voice, the person I became when I let the music take over.

We'd made that music together.

Maybe it was the adrenaline of being so brave so early in the day, but finally, everything went smoothly.

During math, I completed all my assignments on time.

"Did you finish already?" Mr. Taylor asked when I returned the tablet to the back of the room.

"Yes," I said.

He opened his laptop, and I saw his bright blue eyes scanning the screen to double-check my work. His face broke into a giant smile.

"Well done, Soler," he said, giving me two thumbs-up. "There's only one wrong answer, but you've improved so much. If you continue like this, you'll get a badge by the end of the week."

It was about time I got my first badge! Now that I knew how to work on the tablet, I wasn't scared of falling behind anymore.

When the period was over, Tirzah was waiting for me to walk to the next class.

The whole morning, the band members and I looked for each other. Knowing there would be at least one friendly face waiting for me to say hi was enough to help me make it through the next hour and a half.

By the time lunch came, the four of us walked to the cafeteria together. I clutched my lunch bag with the empanadas Papi had packed for me against my chest. Flashbacks from my first day here almost had me bolting away, but I was flanked by my band.

Tirzah was the only one who got school lunch. The pizza looked delicious.

"Do you want to try it?" she asked.

I hesitated, but she started cutting up the giant slice.

"I've never had pepperoni pizza," I said.

"What?" Donovan said.

I shrugged. "I don't like spicy foods."

Beto laughed like I'd told the funniest joke in the world. "Come on, María Emilia," he said. "Pepperoni doesn't even count as spicy."

"To you," I replied. "I've never eaten hot peppers before."

He held the piece of pizza out to me. The scent of cheese mixed with the pepperoni, and the bridge of my nose broke into a sweat.

"Be brave," said Donovan.

What if the pepperoni was ultra hot and my face burst into fire?

I bit down.

My tongue exploded in a delight of flavors. How was this school pizza on the same menu as the atrocious radioactive yellow-cheese sandwich?

"This is almost as good as the one my dad makes," I said. "I'm going to tell him to put pepperoni on his pizza next time."

Donovan shared the enchiladas his mom had sent, and Beto put a container with pupusas in the center of the table. I added my empanadas.

I loved seeing the ripples of delight pass over each one of their faces.

"This is delicious," Tirzah said as she tried one of the empanadas.

"I've never tasted any better," Beto said. "Don't let my abuela hear me say this, but wow."

Donovan didn't seem to be able to speak. He was too busy eating.

I tried a little of everything they shared, and I loved it all.

Lunch with Los Galácticos was so far the best part of school. Instead of sitting by myself or hiding in the library to pretend I wasn't as lonely as I looked, I sat with my friends, exchanging foods from our countries, the foods that made our families happy.

CHAPTER 19

Later that day, we had our first practice. Tirzah picked me up at my house, and together we walked to Donovan's.

Ashley Jane watched from her yard where she was helping her dad mow the lawn.

"Are you and AJ enemies?" Tirzah asked.

I sighed. "We're not exactly enemies . . . She doesn't like me, and I don't know why."

"She doesn't like anyone," Tirzah replied, twirling a pair of drumsticks in the air, as if she were warming up for a workout. "We went to kindergarten together, but when my parents got divorced in fourth grade, she stopped talking to me."

"Why?" I asked.

"I asked her why, and she pretended not to understand my accent . . ."

"But you don't have an accent in English," I said.

"Exactly," she replied.

I wondered about Ashley Jane. What about me threatened her so much she decided I wasn't worthy of being her friend? Her parents and siblings were nice. She was nice to my brothers. I didn't understand.

"Don't worry too much about her," Tirzah said. "Not everyone is going to like you in this life. At least that's something my grandma used to tell me when things like this bothered me too much when I was younger."

"Your grandma rocks," I said. "I don't know what we'd have done without her."

Tirzah smiled. "When she arrived in Utah years ago, she knew no one. Other immigrants like her became her family, and ever since, she's been trying to pay it forward."

I loved that phrase, *pay it forward*. That was also what Celestina was doing with her letters. She'd helped me, from almost a hundred years in the past, without knowing.

Soon, we arrived at Donovan's. His house was a log cabin planted in the middle of an orchard. The sweet twang of apples drifted in the air. A ladder leaned on one of the trees, and a half-full barrel of fruit stood at its side. My mouth watered.

This looked like a fairy tale, and I thought Celestina would've loved it.

"Come on," Tirzah said, leading me to a little door into the garage.

The band was set up inside.

Cardboard boxes and blue-and-yellow plastic bins were heaped against one of the walls. On another there was a huge mural of the Mexican flag intertwined with the American one. A colorful rug was spread on the floor covering the stained cement that still smelled of motor oil and grease.

Against the back wall was the drum set. A giant logo of Cookie the astronaut on top of a flaming meteor was painted on the bass drum, the name *Los Galácticos* underneath it in fancy, curly handwriting.

"Mrs. Sosa painted it," Tirzah said, heading right toward the drums. As soon as she sat down behind the set, she closed her eyes and started beating the drums softly, already lost in a rhythm she seemed to summon from deep in her heart.

Beto stood in front of the electronic keyboard with

headphones on. Today he wore a Real Salt Lake jersey, and a smile cut through the concentration on his face. Cookie lounged on a sofa, licking her paws and washing her face.

I never knew dogs did this just like cats! I blinked a couple of times in case I was imagining the whole thing, but she kept washing her face like my Estrellita would when Violeta and I had a girls' night on a Friday, so long ago it seemed like another life.

She must have felt me looking at her because she looked in my direction and . . . blinked at me.

Goose bumps covered my arms. She was saying she loved me.

"Hola, Emilia! We have a microphone right there," Donovan said, pointing at a rickety table covered with old Oreo wrappers and bottles of water. "Make yourself comfortable."

Part of me was thrilled to be with these cool kids, and another part of me itched to run away. How was this my life? I just sang solos with the school choir. I never imagined I'd be part of a band of misfits: Los Galácticos.

"Why is the band called Los Galácticos? You never told me, Donovan," I asked.

"That's right! I was going to when your brother arrived."

"And his tail was broken."

He laughed so loudly, Tirzah peered at us through narrowed eyes before going back to her drums.

"It all started with my brother, Julián, and his friends Ben and Isaac," he said in a story-telling voice. "They played on the same fútbol team, but before then, they met at ELL class."

"Lucky," I said.

"They started spending all their time together. Isaac noticed that kids kept doing the Vulcan salute to them when they crossed in the hallways."

"The Vulcan salute?"

Donovan demonstrated, lifting his hand, his pinkie and ring fingers glued to each other, a gap, and then the middle finger and index together, the thumb all by itself.

"What's that?" I asked, trying to imitate him and unable to. My middle and ring fingers insisted on sticking together no matter how much I tried.

"The *Star Trek* sign," Beto said, his headphones hooked to his neck for a change.

"*Star Wars*?" I asked.

Donovan laughed. "My brother made the same mistake, and he started a war between two of the greatest fandoms ever that continued all the way to high school. And now college, I guess."

I knew about *Star Wars*, but I'd never even heard of *Star Trek*.

Tirzah, who'd stopped warming up to listen in on the band's origin story, pulled something up on her phone and came over to show me. On her screen there was a picture of a man with pointy ears and black hair in a short bowl cut. "This is Spock. You know, the *Enterprise*? That was the ship."

I shook my head. I mean, I thought I was up to date on movies and general popular culture, and now I felt more like an outsider than ever.

"I feel like an alien. Like I not only came from another country, but another world. I know nothing."

"Exactly!" Donovan said. "Spock and the Vulcans really are aliens. And that's how Julián and his friends felt. And how we all feel at some point when people start talking about something that is supposedly common knowledge or popular culture but we've never heard of it before."

"People in school still call us aliens," Tirzah said. "Sometimes even illegal aliens."

I shivered when I remembered Mateo's little face when one of the Boden boys had asked him for his alien number.

"Were they mad? Julián, Ben, and Isaac?"

Donovan grinned. "Those three are legendary. Instead of getting mad, like everyone expected—you know, because Latinos are violent revolutionaries," he said, rolling his eyes, "they totally embraced the name. They started the band and registered it under the mandatory clubs. The old principal wouldn't let them be The Aliens, so they became Los Galácticos. The principal thought it was because of Real Madrid, but Isaac is a rabid Barcelona fan. He'd never!"

We all laughed at that.

"So we're aliens," I said.

Donovan shrugged. "Especially him." With his lips puckered, he pointed at Beto, who was playing the keyboard with headphones on, eyes closed, swaying to a music only he could hear. The keyboard was unplugged.

We all laughed again, and Beto opened his eyes and, taking his headphones off, said, "So, are we playing or not?"

My palms suddenly prickled with nervous sweat. They'd already heard me sing, but this was the official first rehearsal.

"So what song are we doing?" I asked.

Donovan pointed at a dry erase board with a list of song titles. Mostly pop songs. It had clearly been erased and rewritten many times.

"Those are some of our favorite ones," he said. "But we haven't found the one that really speaks to our audience, you know? Usually, when we've perfected a song, we stream it on our social media, and then the public can vote. It's actually mostly our tías back in our countries and cousins we've never met. None has really taken off, so we're still looking."

"The perfect song will come," Tirzah said, sounding like a sage from the movies.

I stared at the list. I knew a few of the songs but not by heart.

"Lucas left a binder with the lyrics," Tirzah said, guessing my concern. "And remember, you don't really have to sing exactly like the original version. It's not karaoke. We're doing covers. Big difference."

Beto plugged the keyboard in and started playing. Tirzah joined with the beat of the drum. Donovan played the opening chord on his guitar, and before I thought too much about it, I took a deep breath and sang the first line of an *Aladdin* song.

At first my voice was soft and hesitant.

What if Donovan's family said the band couldn't practice anymore because of my horrible voice? What if the band changed their minds?

But as the music took hold of me, I relaxed my shoulders, closed my eyes, and let the rhythm of the song take me.

The words in English applied perfectly to my life, but in a language not my own, there was a little buffer that left some distance, making it easy to tap into my feelings without being overcome by them.

Minutes later, I came back to the room at the sound of applause.

"Bravo!" Donovan's mom exclaimed. "That was amazing!" Her eyes sparkled. "Is this really the first time you all played together? It was like listening to a recording."

Beto shrugged. "Nah, I hit the wrong chord on the second measure. The pitch was too low."

"But she followed it like a wave and matched it!" Mrs. Sosa

said, turning to me. "It's nice to meet you, María Emilia. What a perfect addition you are."

She clicked something on her phone, and soon, my singing voice filled the silence once again. My cheeks burned.

If there was something worse than listening to a recording of my speaking voice, it had to be listening to myself sing. Each time I'd failed to hit a note or breathed in the wrong place, I cringed. But the rest of the band seemed to love it.

Mrs. Sosa said, "After you all watch it and approve, I can post it on the band's YouTube channel. What do you think?"

I wanted to say no. It was one thing to sing with my new friends, in the sacred space of this garage, where the notes of the instruments and my voice made magic, like the combination of the perfect pizza toppings. I had never sung like this in Argentina before. Maybe the experience of leaving everything behind, of having my world turn upside down, was the secret ingredient I needed to literally find my voice.

Finding my voice had come at a high price. I couldn't ignore it or let it go to waste.

"Come on, homes," Beto said, looking around. "The song slaps!"

"Okay," I said, even though I had no idea what 30 percent of his words meant.

We continued singing song after song, but none was as magical as the first one. I treasured the memory and feeling of it like a talisman.

Mrs. Sosa, Karina, made us taquitos and enfrijoladas, which I'd never tried before and were delicious.

Too soon, it was time for me to go back home. My mom picked Tirzah and me up on her way home from work. When she saw us, she said, "You too are glowing like stars. Was the practice a success, then?"

Tirzah smiled. "Here, see it for yourself." She showed Mami the recording that Karina had uploaded on the band's social media channel.

My mom listened to the recording, mesmerized, and when she looked at me, it was like she was seeing a different person. "That was . . . I had no idea you could do that."

She hugged me tightly, and I felt like finally her heart understood what mine wanted to say.

CHAPTER 20

The day after Donovan posted the video, it was as if the invisibility shield around me had vanished.

At the bus stop, Ashley Jane and Kel kept looking at me and gossiping behind their hands. I knew they were competing in the Battle of the Bands too, and judging by their reaction, they must have thought I was a serious threat to them.

"How come you told us she couldn't speak English, AJ?" one of the girls from their group asked. "She sounded perfectly fluent in that song."

I met AJ's eyes to see what she would say, but she just rolled hers and muttered her reply. I caught every word as she said, "Hispanic attention seeker . . . Why won't she go back to where she was born?"

I was stunned to silence as the bus roared up to us. As soon as it was too late to reply, I wished I'd asked if she meant Miami. And even if I hadn't been born in this country, who was she to police who could be here and who couldn't?

Mrs. Contreras had tried to teach me the definition of *comeuppance*. I hadn't really understood the meaning until this moment, when I wanted nothing more than to see AJ get what she deserved for saying something so cruel.

But hoping for something bad to happen to her didn't make me happy. I didn't know a word in any language that described the feelings warring in my heart.

I watched out the window and practiced my song in my mind. Each day, the world tilted closer to the solstice, and I could keep track of the passing of time by the change in the landscape.

Red Ledges had been named for the red rock of its formations that brought visitors from all over the world. But now that fall was finally here, there was another explanation for the name.

The trees seemed on fire, and I had loved watching the leaves turn from amber to bright red and then fall to the ground, where they created a magic carpet on which my brothers and I traveled to imaginary worlds. The willow tree leaves had turned golden and were still holding on to their branches.

The days and weeks went by like the golden-red leaves swirling from the trees. I was still catching up on Utah History and Gov and Civ—everything here was so different from Argentina—but at least I didn't struggle in math anymore. Now when someone in the class needed help with a particularly hard problem, Mr. Taylor asked me to help out.

The band practices were going well too. Our social media views had skyrocketed, and Donovan had started to make the list of books we would order if we won the Battle of the Bands.

"When we win," I corrected him every time.

When I started singing with Los Galácticos, time sped up. Maybe it wasn't that time had stopped for me because I was in the Northern Hemisphere. It had stopped because, without friends, I had put myself on pause. Now every day was filled with activities. And I missed Violeta and Lela, but better yet, I had so many things to tell them when we talked on the phone. I talked to Lela *almost* every day, and I even managed to introduce her to Estrellita one night when Donovan was over.

On Halloween, the band and I dressed up as aliens. We had matching green T-shirts and headbands with googly eyes. I loved sharing a secret only the four of us knew.

As the weather got colder, a little dread starting sneaking into my chest.

Mami still hadn't heard back from the college about extending her contract. She was contracted through the summer, but after that, it was a mystery. The thought of leaving Red Ledges filled me with panic.

If we had to go back to Argentina in August, would I have to do seventh grade a third time?

It would be like being stuck in time, constantly starting over, never finishing anything, leaving parts of me behind open-ended, getting tangled like the fringe of the new scarf Lela had sent me. An even more nightmarish version of that *Groundhog Day* movie.

One afternoon after school, I was doing homework in the

kitchen while Papi cooked a batch of lasagnas. Some families around the neighborhood had hired him to deliver meals a few times a week, and the spinach lasagnas had been his most popular dish so far. By the time the boys and I arrived home from school, Papi had been cooking all day.

I noticed Mateo pacing around the kitchen, looking at Papi and then at me like he was bursting to say something and not knowing how to start.

Finally, when I had to delete the second paragraph of my essay because I kept repeating the same thought, I asked, "Do you need anything, Mati?"

His cheeks went bright red. Was he embarrassed? Papi put the last two trays of lasagna in the oven and turned around to listen to Mateo too.

My brother grinned sheepishly, his pink tongue showing through the gap of his missing teeth. He'd lost about four by now.

"What is it?" Papi asked, drying his hands with his apron.

Mati clasped his hands and gave a big sigh. "Okay, so the teacher said she sent a note, but you haven't answered. You haven't seen it?"

Papi's eyes went wide, and then he slapped his hand on his forehead. "Ay! I saw it, but I didn't read it. And then the alarm for the white sauce went off and I forgot. That was yesterday."

He looked at me, asking for permission to use the computer.

I slid the laptop in his direction, careful that it didn't get dirty with tomato sauce.

Papi checked the email, and then he narrowed his eyes and looked at my brother, who was shrinking and shrinking by the second, hunching his shoulders like he wanted to disappear.

"What happened?" I asked.

By then, Francisco had joined us, his hands full of LEGO pieces. He'd been making a little town for weeks with boxes of LEGO Donovan had brought.

Finally, Papi looked up, and now he was the one who huffed. "Tell me, Mati, why is the teacher asking me to bring a 'traditional Mexican dish' for the Winter Festival next week?"

Mati clenched his teeth in the fakest smile I'd ever seen. "Well, she asked for volunteers for food, and I said I'd bring something from where I'm from."

"And why is she asking me for something Mexican?"

Mateo bit his lip. "Well, that's because when she asked me where I was from, I said Mexico."

"Why?" I asked in surprise.

Papi looked at my brother, giving him the time to come up with an answer.

And then Francisco spoke for him, as if he knew exactly what Mateo's thought process had been. "He said that because it's the easiest, okay?" His voice was shaky, and his eyes teary. "I get tired of correcting everyone that I'm not from Mexico too. I'm from Argentina. No one believes me because they don't know where our accents are from. Neither one of us plays soccer like Messi. Mateo's skin is too dark and his eyebrows are too thick, like that painter Frida's. Right, Mati?"

Francisco put an arm over Mati's shoulder, their eyes shiny with tears. "What's so wrong about going along with what people already think?" Mateo asked.

Papi got on his knees, and my youngest brother went to his arm and hid his face in Papi's shoulder. But I could tell he was crying.

"Ay, Mati, Mati . . ." Papi said. "I love Mexico. I love Spain.

But when people call me Spanish? I correct them because even though I speak Spanish and some of my ancestors were from Spain, I'm not from there. I was born and raised in Argentina."

Mateo shook his head. "You don't understand, Papi. It's hard to explain to people. Mimilia was born here. She has an American passport, and she hates it here—"

"I don't hate it," I said. "Anymore . . ."

The words had come out without thinking, but they were the truth. My brothers and my dad stared at me.

"It's complicated," I said. "I actually like it here now that I finally have friends and I don't feel like a failure because I understand what people are saying."

"Do you love it though?" Francisco asked, challenging me with a tilt of his pointy chin.

"I'm learning to." I wasn't even lying. "It's not home . . . yet. But maybe we don't have to decide now what our ultimate home is, you know?"

Papi winked at me, and then he ruffled Mateo's hair. "No need to look embarrassed, Matu."

Mateo's eyes were downcast. "But when my teacher finds

out I'm not from Mexico, she's going to think I've been lying for months. I corrected her *twice*. She just . . . kept forgetting."

Francisco shrugged. "I mean, when some kids asked me if I'd ever met Messi, I said yes, because remember that one time we went to that restaurant in Mendoza and he'd just left? So his air was still around. It's not exactly a lie, is it?"

We all laughed at that.

"Still, lying, by saying a lie or staying quiet, isn't right." Papi opened a cabinet and brought out his giant recipe book. The one with handwritten notes from generations ago, photocopied pages, yellowing magazine clippings. Like Celestina's binder of letters, except this was his collection of the foods that had fed and comforted our family since time immemorial.

"I'll go to your school tomorrow and explain to the teacher. And then I'll offer to bring a Mexican dish *and* an Argentine one. Do you want to choose?" he asked, offering my brother the sacred recipe book he never allowed us to touch.

A wistful expression passed on Francisco's face, and noticing it, Papi said, "What about you choose something too, Francis?"

Francisco nodded, grateful.

My two brothers hugged Papi and then sat at the table, poring over the recipes, arguing in hushed tones about the pros and cons of alfajores de maicena. Cornstarch cookies filled with dulce de leche were delicious, but they were too time-consuming and messy to make.

Papi looked at me and asked, "Do you want me to make something for your friends too? I mean, since I'm cooking already."

I shrugged. "Sure. Anything you want. My friends already love your cooking."

I told him about the lunch potlucks we had at school every day.

He laughed. "You know, we might all come from different places, have different skin color and political ideologies, but the way to bridge differences hasn't changed that much in the history of the world."

"What do you mean?" I asked, scratching my head with my pencil.

"When languages fail or divide, people come together thanks to food and music."

I thought about one of Celestina's letters from her journey almost a hundred years ago, and then looked at us these last few months. Papi was right.

Food and music brought people together. Even if we couldn't pack everything in our tiny suitcases, sharing the music from my heart while we ate had brought me new friends I never expected.

The scent from the lasagnas filled the kitchen.

And when a few minutes later Mami arrived, our rented house felt like it was giving us all a warm hug. After long years of being empty, it loved having us here.

CHAPTER 21

Band practice with Los Galácticos continued to make time slip by. I worked hard at school, but I really measured time from practice to practice—from the moment I saw Estrellita until the next one. Each day my walk over to Donovan's got chillier. And as the trees became bare, Estrellita started to meet me halfway to Donovan's, happy to trot alongside me. The festival was approaching quickly, and I loved seeing her lie underneath Beto's keyboard as we prepared.

Of course, I should've known that every time things start feeling comfortable, a crisis is right around the corner, waiting. Mine took me by surprise.

One morning, I was in my bed, rehearsing the song that had been playing in my heart for months, when I didn't remember how to say *rainbow* in Spanish.

The realization that I was forgetting my language made me feel sick. I had noticed my brothers—and actually, the whole family—speaking more and more Spanglish and English in the house to make it easier at school. Now I noticed the cost of blending in: losing what made us unique.

I remembered Celestina had gone through a similar thing, and I opened the binder to one of my favorite letters of hers.

Dear Nonna Rosa,

I haven't heard from you since Easter, and now it's almost time for Christmas. Mami was upset because she was asked to bring a traditional dish to the community dinner for Christmas Eve, but her vitel toné didn't turn out the same as back home. My friend Nafiza and her family came to Las Palmas from their new home in Entre Ríos. Her dad makes empanadas árabes. She said he modified a dish from their home to the new flavors and spices he found here, and now everyone loves his lemon beef empanadas. Now that we've both been in Argentina for a while, we can actually communicate in Spanish! Still, she's sad that her little brother is forgetting how to speak in Arabic since there's not a lot of people to practice with and his schoolteacher insists the family help him integrate by speaking Spanish. It's the same with my brothers and little cousins. They speak in Spanish constantly, and I fear they'll forget to speak Neapolitan. What if I forget? I wish there were books in Italian, but the mini library on the teacher's horseback doesn't have anything. I asked Mamma for two books for Christmas: _The Adventures of Pinocchio_ by Carlo Collodi or _Cuore_ by Edmondo De Amicis, but she said she can't find them in Italian.

Since I don't have anything to read in my language, I write to you only in Italian. So I won't forget. You're my link to the Celestina I was back in Napoli. Without her, the one I am today wouldn't exist.

I wish I could see you soon and give you a hug. Maybe next year you'll come join us, Nonna?

With love,
Celestina

In my heart I wished that Celestina and Nonna Rosa had the chance to hug each other again, to sing their songs together.

But when I had read this letter the first time and asked Lela, she had told me that hadn't been the case, sadly. They had never seen each other again.

I held the binder against me, glad to have Castellano to read. Glad that Celestina had letters to connect her back to her grandma. I imagined the links going back in generations in many languages, all of them a song.

Later that day, Mateo came along to band practice with me—our second-to-last before the Battle of the Bands. Francisco was having a birthday dinner with just Mami and Papi. It was all he'd wanted. As a middle child, it was hard for him to get the attention he needed, and he always flew under the radar. The day he'd explained to Papi and me why Mateo had lied to his teacher, it was clear to all of us that Francisco needed some extra love.

But Mateo wasn't too happy about it. We argued the whole walk to Donovan's house, and when we opened the door, a wave of negativity greeted us.

After one look at my friends' grumpy expressions, Mateo said, "I'll stay in the kitchen with Cookie."

"Be good, Mati, and don't make Cookie too hyper, please," I said, eyeing Karina, who was painting another mural in the living room. When she smiled at me, I noticed the blue streak of paint on her cheek.

Mateo nodded and said, "I brought her favorite story." It was his favorite book too, about a police officer with the head of a dog. It was ridiculous and funny.

I ruffled his hair and went to sort out what the argument was all about.

When we made it to the garage, Los Galácticos looked at me and different expressions crossed their faces.

"Finally! The voice of reason," Tirzah said, wrapping an arm over my shoulder.

Donovan's eyes were narrowed. "Don't try to win her over before she knows what this is all about. I don't think she'll agree with you anyway, but whatever."

Beto smiled. "Now I can go back to working on the arrangement. Whatever you decide, you have my vote," he said, and put his headphones on.

Tirzah and Donovan shook their heads.

"Is anyone going to tell me what this is all about?" I asked, dropping my backpack, which landed with a heavy, ominous thud. "Oh no! The tomato marmalade!"

"You brought it?" Donovan said, his eyes glinting with surprise. The argument fell to the wayside in the face of homemade food.

I rummaged in the backpack and took out the jars of tomato marmalade my dad had sent for the band. One extra so we could have it for snacks after we practiced. Luckily none were damaged. The galletas marineras, the homemade crackers, were another story though. Most were broken and pulverized.

"We should have put them in a plastic container instead of a baggy. I'll let Papi know later. In the meantime, we can use regular saltines."

Beto nodded at me, confirming my suspicions that he put those headphones on to pretend he was in his own world, but that in truth he could hear everything we said.

Donovan dashed to the kitchen with his jar of marmalade and a few seconds later came back with a box of saltines, a tub of butter, and a pack of Yoo-hoo drinks.

He handed a sleeve of saltines to each one of us and opened

the jar of marmalade with a satisfying pop. He'd brought little spoons to spread it, and he dropped a tiny bit of marmalade on his finger. "We'll see what this is all about . . ." He licked his finger, and his eyes went so wide I could practically see the fireworks exploding in his mind.

I smiled, delighted. "Your turn," I said to Tirzah and Beto, who'd momentarily left the keyboard to try my dad's famous marmalade.

"I was expecting it to be more like ketchup," Beto confessed, and we all started laughing.

"No wonder you didn't want to try it!" I exclaimed.

He shrugged and made a cracker and marmalade sandwich. "But since you were always brave trying what we brought to share, it was only fair we gave it a chance."

Tirzah's crackers were gone. She rubbed her tummy. She was wearing a reindeer T-shirt that said *The OG Unicorns*. "Good thing I don't have to sing," she said. "I'm so full now."

I pursed my lips. "That's why I'm not eating until after practice," I said. "Now that you're all fed and happy, tell me what you were all fighting about."

Tirzah and Donovan exchanged a look, and Beto said, "See you later!" and went back to his keyboard.

Donavan spoke first. "Tirzah had a great idea . . . You know the song you keep singing when you think no one can hear you? What if we play that one for the Battle of the Bands?"

My face felt like I was on fire, and the feeling spread to my whole body as his words sank in.

"My song? But it's not finished yet . . ." I hadn't been afraid to hum it around the band members, but I had never really shared it with them.

Tirzah's cheeks were red as well, but she said, "I love how happy you are when you sing it, María Emilia. I can tell the lyrics mean a lot to you, so the boys and I made this arrangement."

"You made a what?" I asked.

Instead of explaining, the three of them played the same melody I'd been humming for months on their instruments. I'd never heard one of my own songs played by someone else. All that was missing was my voice. Was I ready to share this part of me with them?

But then I remembered my desire to pay it forward. To find a way for my story to help someone else.

What better way to send a message out to the world than a song that had come straight from the heart? Celestina had her letters, and I had my songs. Each one of us had found a way to record our story. Who knew? Perhaps a hundred years in the future, a descendant of Los Galácticos would sing this song when they felt like an alien.

First I sang it softly, but before I knew it, the song broke free.

In the end, my friends surprised me by repeating the last line—*those you love are never far*—in Spanish and Portuguese. Beto rapped in a language I'd never heard before, but it was so powerful, that when his last note rang, it still echoed on the walls.

"What was that?" I asked, tears stinging my eyes.

Leaving the drums, Tirzah placed a placating hand on my arm and said, "Okay, I'm going to tell you the whole story . . . This is what happened." She sat on the sofa and wrapped herself in one of the rebozos that were there in a pile. "I was home last night, and my grandma was on the computer with my cousin Becca from Rio. I was singing your song in my room. I hadn't picked up all the lyrics, but you always sing that one line. I didn't know it carried all the way to the kitchen. But later, my grandma told me that Becca cried even though she couldn't tell what the words said. I roughly translated it into Portuguese for her. She loved it and said that you must sing a verse in Spanish, and I in Portuguese. And then when I came over and told these two, Beto said that he could say a few things in Garifuna so his family knew what he really felt, and I had an idea."

Even before she finished speaking, my heart had already started hammering.

No, no, no, no . . .

It was one thing to share this song with my family and my friends. But it was another to sing it in front of everyone. It would be like placing my naked heart out in the open.

Donovan and Tirzah exchanged a look. Even Beto took his headphones off and came over to the sofa and sat next to me. He patted my shoulder, and I realized that I was already crying.

"I guess that's a no, then," he said.

I never wanted to let people down. These were my friends.

I trusted them, but they'd expected too much. They hadn't even left me with enough time to decide.

"We're not doing it if it affects you so much," Tirzah said with a glare at Donovan. "I knew it was too late to ask. Forget we even mentioned it. Forget it."

"But why would you say no, María Emilia?" Donovan asked.

I looked up at my band. A few months ago, we lived in different countries, different continents, each living their separate lives. And now?

They were my family. And in a family, we had to open up. More than anything, I wanted them to understand what I'd been going through all this time.

"It's not finished," I said. What I meant was *It's not perfect*.

I realized that expecting to do everything perfectly, without giving myself room to fail, had stolen a lot of joy from my life. But I didn't know how to break that cycle.

I had finished the song, but I was scared they wouldn't like it.

Sometimes when we move between worlds and languages, faiths, families and timelines, what comes out first is the essence of who we are. It doesn't need to be perfect. It is what it is. But it was hard not to see all my flaws.

Beto said, "I have an idea: Think about it. We still have one more practice to finalize whatever we decide to play. Tomorrow, you can let us know what you decide."

"It's your song, María Emilia," Tirzah said. She kissed me and hugged me tightly. "But remember it speaks to us because you put into music what none of us could express before." She stood. "Now. Let's practice everything else just in case."

We played in harmony together until Estrellita snuffled her way into our little group. I pulled her in for a snuggle as Mateo peeked inside the garage. Her fur felt oddly stiff under my hand. "Ready to go, Mimilia?" His face was so sleepy.

I gave the puppy one more squeeze and said, "Yes, Mati. Ready."

Now that it was almost winter, the sun went down around five in the afternoon. The days seemed so short and dark. At seven, it looked like it could be midnight.

I grabbed my brother's hand, but before we left, Donovan said, "Emilia! Before you leave, I wanted to ask you something . . . not about the song. It's something else."

"Go ahead," I said, putting my notebook with the lyrics inside my backpack.

Donovan looked at Mateo and grinned. "So, the thing is, I'm sure you noticed my mom started painting the mural in the living room. Well, Cookie's going bonkers with the sensory overload."

Cookie whined, like she did every time someone discussed her mischief making, and then lay at my feet.

I petted her and noticed again that her hair was all stiff. "What is it?"

That's when Karina peeked in and said, "This morning when I was prepping the walls, she thought the paint was like makeup or something. I painted the first layer, and the house phone rang. I usually let it go to voice mail, but then I wondered if it was Julián calling. It was telemarketers after all, but when I came back, Cookie was acting super guilty."

"Like when she pulled that whole platter off the counter last week. Remember, Mimilia?" Mateo said, shaking his finger at Cookie. She'd been coming over to visit whenever Donovan did.

"The whole right side of her body was covered in cream paint. It's not washable, and I can't use thinner on her." Karina sighed. "That's going to take forever to come off."

"You can't have her around when you're painting," I said.

"Duh," said Mateo.

"Could you keep her at your house for a few days?" Donovan asked, clutching his hands in front of him like he was praying.

I shook my head and his smile vanished, but then I laughed. "Of course! She can come over anytime."

Cookie seemed to understand the whole conversation. She sat in front of me and then plopped on her back for Mateo to rub her tummy.

We all laughed again.

When Mami drove over to pick us up, she was smiling from ear to ear at the sight of Cookie. "We've missed you . . ." Then she wrinkled her nose. "Stinky girl! What's that smell?"

"Paint," I said, sitting in the front seat while my brother and Cookie sprawled in the back seat.

Mami always turned the music off when we were in the car

so we could talk, but today I had too many things in my heart and stayed quiet.

Now I didn't miss our home in Mendoza like I was a person walking around without a part of her heart. My brothers were safe and happy. Papi hadn't perfected his pizza, but the new version had pepperoni, which was delicious. I wasn't on the cheer squad, but I was in Los Galácticos, and although Ashley Jane continued to pretend like I didn't exist, at least she'd stopped calling me names. And the cherry on top was that Cookie was with me for at least a week.

The real problem was, there was a song trapped inside me. A song that showed my whole heart, and I was afraid to share it.

Although the sky was a dark blue, there was always a glow of light right at the end of the road. Papi had said it was the lights from Saint George, but I thought it was a reminder that there was light at the end of the desert if we only remembered to look ahead instead of behind us, at the past.

CHAPTER 22

That night, my brothers fought over who'd get to sleep with Cookie. When the argument reached the tears and accusations point, Papi intervened.

"Now," he said, "remember she's a guest. Would we be fighting like this if Lela were here?"

But neither one of my brothers wanted to give up.

"I'll take her with me," I said, heading to my attic room.

Now Mateo and Francisco groaned and made me the object of their complaints.

"It's not fair!" Mateo said. "It was my idea for her to come over."

"It was not!" I said.

"Was too!" he replied. "I said to Donovan's mom that we could take Cookie."

"Well," Francisco interrupted, "I feel like she should sleep in my bed because it's my birthday . . ."

Finally, Mami declared, "She won't sleep in anyone's bed. Last time she slept upstairs, she barked all night at every single car that drove by and woke up Lilly Ann Boden. Cookie ate the leavening rolls dough, and she annihilated Mateo's snow boots."

"But she didn't know any better!" I said.

The truth was, tonight I wanted to be with a friend and tell her all about my fears without feeling judged. Maybe she had some extra stardust power to help me get over my fears and insecurities.

Papi didn't look like he'd budge, but I insisted. "I'll leave my door closed all night, Papi!"

Mami shook her head. "If she gets out, who knows what trouble she'll find in this house . . ."

"The Jensens will come back and hunt us!" Francisco exclaimed.

"Haunt us," Mami corrected him, obviously trying to keep a straight face.

"She'll stay in the laundry room," Papi said. "It's nice and warm in there, and it's a small room she can protect without having to bark all night."

No one but my parents seemed satisfied with the arrangement. My little brothers weren't happy to leave Cookie behind, but they finally gave in.

I went back to doing my homework in the kitchen next to Mami, who was correcting essays for her students. Finals were coming up, and she wanted to return the papers the next day so her students had time to prepare.

After bedtime stories, Papi came back to check on us.

Mami turned a page in the stack of papers in front of her, and she yawned loudly.

"Are you okay, Mami?" I asked.

She rubbed her tired eyes. "I need to call it a night. I'm not built for staying up until all hours anymore."

Papi scratched his face and looked at the clock on the kitchen wall. "It's not even eleven, and we're already too tired to stay up. I guess we're assimilating."

Assimilating. Blending in. Were we really losing part of our culture?

"Now, if only I could get up earlier than six, then I'd believe you," Mami said.

"That's still only seven hours of sleep, Mami," I said, rubbing my own eyes too. "You're being too hard on yourself."

Mami gave me a smile and nodded. "You're true, Emilia."

"You mean I'm right?"

She laughed. "We're all too tired to talk in English or Spanish. Let's go to bed."

Cookie's chin had rested on my feet while I worked on history. I was determined to catch up on this subject that had always been my best but was now my most challenging one. It felt like completely starting over.

Mami kissed me on the head, and then she and Papi headed to their room.

"Don't stay up too late, and please leave Cookie in the laundry room."

I nodded.

In reality, I had intended to obey, like I would've in another life. But when I was done writing the summary of the chapters on Utah history to share with Tirzah, I saw Cookie's face, and I couldn't send her into the laundry room on her own. Like me, she looked like she didn't want to be alone.

"Shh, quiet," I said, and she quietly padded up the stairs behind me.

She walked around the room, sniffing the corners, inspecting every inch to see what was new.

She then stood on her little hind legs and looked out the window. I followed her gaze and to my surprise saw snowflakes as big as my hand fluttering through the glow of the streetlights. The snow had already started accumulating down in the yard. It looked so eerie and beautiful.

Cookie whined.

"We can't make any wishes tonight," I said, hoping the clouds would break for a second so I could get a glimpse of a star. So I could wish to remember who I was supposed to be.

Cookie licked my hand.

"I know! I can make a wish on you! After all, regardless of the name that silly boy gave you, you're a little star and you'll be my own little star forever and ever."

The words sparked a thought, and I grabbed my notebook and scribbled quickly.

The last and final verse of my song came out in a rush, and when I was done writing, I was proud of myself. It wasn't perfect, but it showed what I really felt:

> I wished upon a stray
> Who came to me disguised as a star.
> She reminded me that bonds can stretch,
> Love can change even the most hardened heart,
> Like the ocean or the wind
> You can't contain it.
> Let it fly and reach the rainbow.
> Don't forget
> That those you love are never far.

Satisfied with my work, I made sure my door was closed. Then I set an alarm for a little earlier than Mami's so I could have Cookie down in the laundry room before the rest of the family woke up and realized I had disobeyed.

It was just the one night.

Tomorrow I'd feel better, and I wouldn't need the comfort of my borrowed dog, or at least that's what I told myself.

Maybe knowing that Cookie loved me unconditionally made me feel better. I went to bed and had a dreamless night with her pressed to my side.

When I woke up, it was to absolute silence, and an empty spot beside me. I frantically looked at the clock and saw it was seven thirty.

I jumped from the bed.

I had slept through my alarm! Which meant Mami had slept in too because otherwise she'd have come to wake me up.

"Cookie!" I called.

But no puppy came over to reassure me. With horror, I realized the door of my room was open.

I darted downstairs. But she wasn't in the laundry room, or with the boys.

In the kitchen, I found the stack of Mami's essays scattered all over the table. My heart sputtered and then started racing.

What had Cookie done?

But I didn't have time to worry about her when Mami had a big day ahead of her.

The microwave clock blinked 00:00. The power must have

gone out in the night. I tried one of the light switches, and fluorescent light illuminated the dog-less kitchen.

I gathered the papers to pretend nothing had happened with them, and then I went into my parents' room to wake Mami up.

"Mami," I whispered. "We slept in. It's seven forty-five."

Mami sat up in the bed like a windup toy. "Seven forty-five?"

She didn't waste a second before she ran to the bathroom.

Papi sat up too and checked the clock on the nightstand. "Oh no," he said. "The power must have gone out and the alarms . . ."

Mami came out of the bathroom, already dressed, with no makeup on but her hair arranged into a careful bun on the nape of her neck. "How do I look?"

"Tired, but that's what coffee's for," Papi said. "Although if the power's gone, I guess there's no fresh coffee today."

Mami kissed him and then hugged me tightly for a second or two. "Thanks for saving my life, mi amor. I owe you big-time."

She dashed out before I could tell her about the essays.

Soon, the sound of tires on new snow told me Mami was on her way out. I dashed to the window to watch her carefully drive on the freshly salted streets.

"At least the roads are okay," Papi said, going through notifications on his phone. "But it looks like the boys will have a snow day today."

My heart hammered thinking of Cookie. I needed to go to the shed and see if that's where she'd headed. If she wasn't there, where could she be?

Donovan had trusted me with her, his beloved brother's dog. Julián had been nothing but super nice to me. Mami had called me her savior, but all I had done was lie.

"Oh, wait," Papi said, checking his phone. "There's a two-hour weather delay for you, actually. So we have two extra hours this morning." The universe was giving me a chance to fix the mess I had made.

"I'm going to get ready for the day," Papi said. "And then we can make pancakes or waffles. What do you think?"

"I'm not that hungry," I said.

He placed a hand on my forehead. "Are you okay? You never turn down pancakes!"

I wanted to tell him about Cookie, but what if I made him worry and then I found her and it was all for nothing?

Before I replied with another lie, he went to change. While

my brothers still slept, I went back to my room. I put on my tennis shoes and a big jacket and headed out.

My heart jumped when I saw Cookie-sized paws prints in the snow, leading to the shed.

But when I opened the door, all I saw was the poor deer watching me with glassy eyes.

"Cookie," I called, but there was only silence and the smell of musty, old places. "Cookie," I tried again.

My heart beating frantically, I went back out, heading toward the circle of naked willow trees, following the paw prints.

I went around the block, calling her over and over. Until I came face-to-face with Ashley Jane.

She had a giant shovel in one hand, and she'd been heading to my driveway.

She saw the dog treat in my hand and probably the anguished expression on my face. "Is she lost?" she asked.

I nodded.

"When?" she asked.

"I don't know. She must have opened the door. She'll chase absolutely anything . . ."

There was a heavy silence, and then she asked, "Do you want me to help you look for her?"

This was the girl who'd accused me of stealing her favorite shirt. The one who'd made up stories that I couldn't speak English. The one who'd called me a *Hispanic attention seeker* all because I had dared to sing from my heart.

Why would she be nice to me now?

What if she went to Donovan and told him I'd lost his dog? His brother, Julián, would be home for Christmas. What would he say when he found out I'd been so careless?

I shook my head. "No, thanks. I'm sure she's waiting for me at home."

I looked over my shoulder, and Mateo and Francisco were standing by the window. Something in their expression told me they knew Cookie was lost.

Without another word to my neighbor, I headed back inside. I felt Ashley Jane watching me all the way to my door.

When I walked in, Mateo asked, "Where is she? You went on a walk, but where is she?"

I shook my head and swallowed my tears.

My sweet wishing star was lost.

CHAPTER 23

Papi and the boys helped me look for Cookie around the neighborhood without knowing it was my fault she was lost. Mateo and Francisco plodded in their uncomfortable but toasty boots. At first I didn't mind the cold seeping through my tennis shoes, until my feet became blocks of ice and I couldn't walk anymore.

Papi's cheeks were red with the cold. As the snow started falling again, his phone chimed. When he checked it, he said, "School is totally canceled for the day. Why don't you call Donovan and see if Cookie made her way back to their house?"

Although the idea had been floating in my mind ever since I'd discovered she was gone, I recoiled when he said it aloud.

"Papá! I can't call him and tell him I lost his dog! He trusted me! He . . ."

My chin was quivering, and Papi, who could never watch me cry, hugged me and said, "Once Mami is back from school, we'll drive around and find her."

"Can we call the shelter?" I asked. "Last time she got lost, Donovan said she ended up in the shelter because she keeps wiggling out of her collar and her microchip wasn't working."

Papi shivered. Mateo had taken his hat. "Okay, let's go home and get warm, and then we'll plan."

The boys took hot bubble baths, but I couldn't sit still knowing Cookie was out in this storm. My feet throbbed with the pain of coming back to normal room temperature, and I thought of her tender paws, unused to being out in the cold, and how confused she must be all alone.

After the boys were out of their baths, Papi started making lunch, and I took the chance to jump into a hot shower. I headed downstairs in time to see Mami walking in.

"I thought I'd never make it back!" she said, hugging me.

"But you're home early!" I said.

Mami bit her lower lip and shook her head. "The students

are used to snow here, but this was a blizzard. It's a good thing no one showed up to class because I went through the tests one more time to make sure I'd squeezed in all the credit I could for the dear ones, and I realized there was a page missing from one. I can't believe I lost it! I feel horrible."

My heart jumped to my throat.

I had to tell Mami what had really happened.

My parents hadn't really expected me to be perfect. All my life, they'd seen me make mistake after mistake. What they expected from me was to learn from my mistakes.

I took a deep breath and confessed. "Mami, last night I let Cookie sleep in my room. I closed the door, and I put my backpack in front of it, but she opened it anyway." I couldn't meet her eye yet. "This morning I saw she'd scattered your papers all over the place. I tried to put them in a pile so you wouldn't notice, but I guess I missed one. It wasn't your fault."

Mami pressed her lips.

"The worst is that she's gone, and it's all because of me." My voice cracked.

"But she had never left the house in the middle of the night when she was here," Mami said in a soft voice. "Why would she run away, especially when a storm was coming?" I thought of my little Estrellita back home, who had done the same thing the night I got our life-changing news. It felt like more proof of the connection between my darling cat and this hyper pup who failed companion dog school.

"Have you called Donovan to ask if she's there?" Mami asked.

"I'm scared," I admitted.

Mami kissed my forehead. "I know it can be scary, but telling the truth is always the best policy, mi amor. Maybe you're worried for nothing . . ."

"If she's not there, would you drive me to the shelter? Remember that guy on the radio saying how many animals turn up in the county shelter after a storm?"

"Let's call first," she said. "The roads are a bedlam."

I didn't know the word *bedlam*, but the roads during this snow could only be chaos.

I was so nervous I couldn't even eat, and when my parents were softly whispering in the family room, I headed to my own room to text Donovan from my mom's phone. I didn't dare call him in case he could hear the panic in my voice.

Hey, how are things? This storm is wild, no?

My heart pounded as I waited for a reply.

But when the seconds went on and on, I started worrying that Cookie had shown up and he was too mad to tell me anything.

I texted Tirzah and Beto too.

I'm catching up on schoolwork, Tirzah replied. *See you tonight at practice? We can't miss our last rehearsal.*

I typed, *Are you sure Donovan can make it? I texted him and he never replied.*

She sent me a rolling eyes emoji and said, *He's shoveling snow in the neighborhood. His brother and Beto's always did the driveways of the little old ladies around the corner.*

So Donovan wasn't avoiding me.

Still, I didn't know what to do.

When I was getting ready for another round of looking for Cookie, Mami came into my room.

"Is she back?" I asked.

Mami made a pouty face. "No, I'm sorry."

"Oh," I said, my hopes deflating. "What is it, then?"

"Fantastic news," she said, and sat on the bed next to me. "I found the missing page in my backpack. I'd never taken it out and almost missed it completely. It belongs to this girl, a student from Puerto Rico who's been very homesick these last few weeks. I felt she wasn't trying hard enough anymore. I didn't know how else to encourage her to continue. Then I read her paper. It was so promising, but unfortunately, it ended without a conclusion. I wanted to know what her plans for the future are now that she found her reason for being."

"That last page!" I said, dismayed.

Mami nodded. "I was so worried about what to do. I didn't want to fail her. Not when her writing came straight from her heart and showed so much potential. But at the same time, I couldn't give her a passing grade when she apparently hadn't finished the assignment."

That heaviness fell down to my stomach. "What if you never found the other page . . ." I couldn't even complete the sentence. I felt so bad for that poor student.

"But I found it, and the rest of the essay is a song of triumph. She talks about finally letting her heart soar. About letting herself fail because, like a fledgling learning how to fly, it's inevitable that you'll fall at some point or another. But you're not made to remain in the nest. You're meant to beat your wings, open your beak, and offer your best squawk into the world. Isn't that lovely?"

Mami's face had become excited as she gesticulated with her hands.

I had a hunch the essay hadn't only helped the student.

Then Mami's eyes became velvety soft, and she said, "I've missed the voice of our pajarita . . ."

"But I sing all the time. Even in English, and you know I hate my accent."

Mami was still smiling sadly. "Why would you hate that part of yourself? Did you know that even birds have accents? A nightingale in Europe sounds different from one in America, but it's still the same beautiful song."

"I hate my accent, and at the same time I'm scared of losing my accent in Spanish, Mami." I'd finally confessed my greatest fear. "Or even losing my Spanish completely. Like Celestina's family lost the Italian language."

"We might have lost the Italian language, but we didn't lose the music in it. Ever wondered why Argentines speak the way they do? We retained the music of the words. And even in Spanish, you can find words from the Arabic and the

Indigenous people who live in Argentina. Languages evolve. They assimilate to changes. Remember, pajarita, even if you don't know it, your heart sings in more than one language. Your blood roars in a multitude of voices, and although you don't speak Italian like Celestina, or the languages of your other abuelas and abuelos, the mark of their voices is still in your soul."

Maybe it was the truth in her words, or the love in her voice, or maybe it was that she understood my heart. Tears welled up in my eyes.

"Thank you, Mamá," I said. "Now, I need to find Cookie, our band's mascot, so we can win Battle of the Bands."

CHAPTER 24

I went out to look for Cookie one more time before I had to head to Donovan's and confess I'd lost his brother's dog and the band's mascot. All I could see in my mind was the logo of Cookie with an astronaut bubble helmet around her head, her tongue lolling out.

I smiled through the tears, which hadn't stopped now that they'd started. I didn't know how to contain them, but a part of me was tired of pushing against a cracking dam anyway.

When I was about to turn back home, I heard someone call, "María Emilia!"

I recognized that voice.

The girl who'd cancel me without giving me the chance to say hi: Ashley Jane.

My knees started shaking. Not because I was scared of her,

but because I couldn't pretend I had it all together when I was in front of her.

She seemed to have X-ray vision, seeing through my filters, the pretension, the show I put on for everyone else. I'd been so good at pretending to be perfect, I'd even fooled my parents, who were the smartest people I knew. Maybe what I disliked most about Ashley Jane . . . was that I worried she was right.

And now we stood face-to-face, as the sun dipped behind the mountains and the frigid air snaked inside my soul despite Lela's cozy scarf.

"Hi, Ashley Jane," I said. This time, the *j* sound came out perfectly.

She couldn't hide the look of surprise that passed over her face.

"Hi," she said, and her voice was so soft. "I need to show you something."

I didn't know if I could trust her, but I wasn't going to run away anymore.

There were so many things I wasn't perfect at, but I'd always been brave, and I wasn't about to break the streak now.

Ashley Jane was a girl just like I was. Why had I given her so much power over me?

I followed her. Quietly, we walked side by side to her house. My brothers had played here pretty much every day since we'd arrived, but I'd never even gone inside.

Ashley Jane led me through the side door. The house was warm and fragrant with the scent of cinnamon. My stomach growled, reminding me I hadn't eaten anything all day. I'd been too worried about Cookie.

"There she is," Ashley Jane said, and pointed to a nest made of big pillows and blankets in the corner of the den. In the center of the nest rested Cookie in the shape of a crescent.

I gasped and rushed over. "Is she okay?" I asked, kneeling in front of her and petting her head. She had a bandage around one of her back paws.

Cookie opened her eyes briefly and blinked at me, like my kitty used to do. She wiggled her little butt, like she was saying she was okay, but then went back to sleep.

"She's okay, I think, but she was limping when I saw her earlier today."

I turned to look at Ashley Jane. "When and where did you find her, and why didn't you come get me immediately?"

Her face went a bright red, and she shrugged. "I saw her at

the gas station, circling around like she was waiting for some-one. I waited to see if you, Donovan, or any of your other friends was around, but then Alex, the gas station owner, said he hadn't seen any of you. He said he got some of that Yoo-hoo stuff you guys love . . ." She rolled her eyes. "But Alex said he'd been feeling a little sad all day with the snowstorm and people getting stuck, and Cookie? Is that her name?" I nodded and she continued. "Cookie kept him company, even though he felt bad she didn't have her collar on, and he couldn't call you or Donovan. But when Cookie saw me, she wanted to come back with me."

"Why didn't you bring her to my house? I've been frantic with worry."

Ashley Jane's face was red again. "I didn't want to bring her to you hurt. I brought her here to wrap up her paw first."

"She's not used to walking in the snow," I said.

Ashley Jane nodded. "She sat at my feet and slept for a long time. Every time I wanted to go across the street to get you, she would pull me by my shirt and bring me back here to this room. My mom said that when she was done sleeping, the dog would come get you, but then . . . I heard you calling, and I was worried about you."

Her words bounced between us for a while, until they finally sank in.

"You were worried about me? But I thought you hated me . . ." I said.

She didn't deny it.

And in that moment, I realized I didn't need her to apologize to me, but I needed to apologize to her. "I'm sorry that first day we met your mom gave me your favorite shirt," I said. "I wanted to give it back and not have it turn into a mess like it eventually did. I'm so sorry."

AJ shrugged. "I'm the one who messed everything up." She looked down at her feet. "That shirt didn't even fit me anymore, and I don't know why I reacted the way I did. I was scared that you were hanging out with the coolest kids at school . . . I'm so sorry. I hope that you stay here in Red Ledges. I hope we have a chance to be friends, even after all that happened."

She finally looked up at me, and I gave her a soft smile. "Thanks. I hope so too."

And as if she'd been waiting for Ashley Jane and me to fix our issues, Cookie opened her eyes, yawned, stood on wobbly legs, and headed toward the door.

"Did she really orchestrate this whole thing?" Ashley Jane asked, sounding as awed as I felt.

I looked at this angel dog, this meteoric comet that had watched out for me since my first day here. I still didn't know if she was the reincarnation of my dear cat, or if their angel souls were friends in heaven. Either way, they both wanted me to realize that love is all that matters.

Not perfection. Not appearances. Just love.

I looked at my watch. It was almost time for band practice. "I have to go now," I said, "but will you be at the festival tomorrow?"

My heart pounded. No matter her answer, I'd done my part. I couldn't judge her either way, but still, when she smiled and nodded, my heart soared.

"I will," she said.

Beaming, I headed back to my house, Cookie trailing behind me.

CHAPTER 25

Instead of telling Donovan the truth about Cookie's disappear-
ance, the first thing I did was share my decision about the
song: that we should sing my original just as they'd thought. I
shared the full song with them, as if I could delay telling the
truth about Cookie.

> *The mountain is hard to climb*
> *When you think you're all alone.*
> *In the darkness, the wind blowing,*
> *The doubts are louder,*
> *The fear is stronger.*
> *Just extend your hand and you'll find*
> *Those you love are never far.*
> *Across oceans, mountains, rivers,*

Years or worlds apart,

In spite of death,

Love knows no end.

The bonds can stretch,

But they won't break unless you forget

That those you love are never far.

After the rain,

The rainbow is always there

To remind you that those you love are never far.

Brighter days are on the way

And the tears of yesterday, like the rain,

Cleansed the path you walk today.

I wished upon a stray

Who came to me disguised as a star.

She reminded me that bonds can stretch,

Love can change even the most hardened heart,

Like the ocean or the wind

You can't contain it.

Let it fly and reach the rainbow.

Don't forget

That those you love are never far.

The last refrain stayed the same in each of the languages my bandmates added, and we practiced and practiced until each note synched perfectly, each chord rang true, and we could each play and sing with our eyes closed, assured we were in perfect harmony.

"I love the finished lyrics, Emilia!" Donovan said after we nailed a second rendition in a row.

If I closed my eyes, I could see the magic of our music still floating in the air. The song was a million times better when Tirzah, Donovan, and Beto added their refrain in Portuguese, Spanish, and Garifuna.

The rest of the band celebrated with the pupusas Beto's grandma had sent, and although my stomach growled with hunger, I couldn't eat. Guilt occupied the whole space in my belly. When it had been time for the chorus in Spanish, I took a deep breath, but I couldn't do it. The words froze on my tongue.

But when Donovan asked about Cookie's first night at my house, I knew there was no other choice but to tell the truth.

"Actually, the little stinker opened the front door and ran out. She wandered around the neighborhood, probably fulfilling wishes all night long. Then she ended up at Ashley Jane's, so I went in the house and finally talked to her."

Los Galácticos looked at me as if I'd grown a second head.

"You what?" Donovan asked.

I shook my head. "It's all fixed between us. I mean, it doesn't mean we'll be best friends, but at least we don't hate each other anymore."

"No," Donovan said. "You lost Cookie and you didn't call me?"

My cheeks were flaming. "I'm sorry . . ."

He shook his head. "Listen, Emilia, I trusted you with my brother's dog."

Instead of accepting his accusations, I snapped. "You've lost her before. Don't pretend like it hasn't happened to you, okay?"

He shook his head and wouldn't talk to me anymore. The magic of my song dissolved as I packed up my things.

Great. I had made my peace with Ashley Jane, and now Donovan and I would be estranged because of an accident?

All night long, I went over the fight with Donovan in my mind. I tried to concentrate on the song, but I was still scared, and I felt no peace because I'd let my friend down.

Before I was ready it was the morning of the show. I stayed in bed as long as I could, hoping to instead wake up on Sunday when it would all be over.

But Cookie came to get me, limping all the way upstairs, and looked at me with an expression that said that when we fall, we get up. When we let friends down, we fix it up.

I threw my covers aside and got ready for the show.

The community center was packed. Karina, Donovan's mom, was at the ticket booth.

"We're running out of tickets!" she said, her smile going from ear to ear. "I had to send Julián to get me more."

"Julián is in town?" I said, my cheeks flaring at the thought of Cookie's rightful owner, and the OG Los Galácticos creator, listening to us perform.

Karina smiled even wider than before. She was positively glowing with happiness.

My brothers and my parents had saved us seats in the second row, as far up front as they could, and I went to kiss them one last time before it was my time to go onstage.

"Remember to sing with your heart, pajarita," Papi said.

My brothers gave me the thumbs-up, and I left, my legs shaking.

Backstage, I stood with my band members, Los Galácticos, dressed in our Halloween costumes. These aliens that had taken me in like a family.

"No matter what, let's have fun first. Okay?" said Beto, whose serious side always emerged during the most critical times.

"Donovan . . ." I said.

Tirzah and Beto sent him a charged look, and Donovan's face softened.

"I'm sorry," I said, my voice already wobbly. "I didn't want you to know I'd made a mistake. But we're friends, and we're a band, and I should have told you."

He pressed his lips. "I'm the one who's sorry. The important thing is that Cookie is safe now. Thanks to you."

With relief, I rushed in for a hug, and Tirzah and Beto piled in behind me. I was still squeezed in the group hug when the principal announced our name and the charity we had chosen to sponsor: the book mobile.

I followed my band onstage. Ashley Jane and her mom

were sitting right behind my family. I waved at her, and she waved back.

The audience applauded for a few seconds, and then there was deep silence.

In the movies they say that before your death, your life flashes in front of your eyes. Turns out it also does when your life is going to change forever, when you're about to become a new person and need to tell the old you that everything will be okay. As I held my entire past in my heart, I finally felt my sorrow melt into gratitude because, without all those difficulties, I never would've made it so far.

I said thank you to the old María Emilia, who would forever be part of me. I was excited to see what I would become, without the pressure of expectations.

Donovan played the first chords. Tirzah followed with the beat of her drums, and immediately, my heart echoed it. Beto played the melody on the keyboard and gave me my note.

I took a deep breath and made my voice ring.

At first, I panicked, knowing that I was slightly off pitch, my voice too timid to take up space. I went back inside my mind and closed my eyes.

I let my heart take over and pushed on.

The change was electric, like a current running all the way from my heart to the hearts of all the people in the audience.

I let the melody take me, smiling through the tears welling in my eyes. But I blinked them away because I wanted to remember this sight forever.

Then the chorus arrived, and Tirzah sang her piece in Portuguese, her voice clear as a bell. Beto joined in words that sounded like a lullaby. Donovan sang looking at his brother, sitting in the audience and mouthing the words back at him. Before I lost my courage, I sang.

In Spanish. With words from all my ancestors and the people that had built my country.

In the Spanish of my Mendoza accent, that carried the music of forgotten mother tongues. The accent that sounded nothing like the one from Buenos Aires that people kept expecting, but one that I was proud of.

It was the sound of my heart, what I spoke in my dreams when there was no one to impress.

By the time the second line in the chorus came around, the whole audience was clapping and singing along.

The guitar and keyboard went silent. Tirzah clapped with her drumsticks, and everyone clapped and sang, in a cacophony of sounds, the audience off-key and off tempo, but all united in letting our hearts speak truth.

And in that truth, we were all the same, united.

EPiLOGUE

My family gathered around the computer as Lela, Tía Yoana, and Violeta gave us the news. "Make room for us! In a couple of weeks, we'll be there to spend New Year's with you!" Lela exclaimed.

"Mami!" I exclaimed, shocked that my parents had kept this surprise from me.

"And we're bringing your lost suitcase, Mimilia!" Violeta said, moving the screen so I could see my battered little suitcase. It was covered in airline stickers. "It arrived a couple of days ago."

I started singing with joy, while Cookie, who we were dog-sitting for the weekend, jumped around me on her two hind legs.

My brothers ran to make a bed for Lela, Tía, and Violeta. But I totally intended to have many sleepover nights with my grandma, my aunt, and my cousin in the attic room. The whole family celebrated long after our phone chat was over. Celestina had never seen her grandma again, but I would get to see mine.

Later that night, I sat by my window, wearing my Galácticos shirt, rubbing Cookie's ears, and watching the stars blinking in the sky, and found Celestina's Polaris. I'd had my dad point out the star my great-great-grandma had wished upon so many times before she immigrated, so that I could always find it. I was part of her wishes come true.

I'd sung my song, and even so many generations later, her feelings and dreams still lived in me. Just as the stars were eternal compared to the briefness of humans' lives, her wishes turned into music had reached me, all these years later.

And as if that weren't enough, I had a little star of my own who I knew would always be with me . . . one way or another.

Those we love are never far . . .

ACKNOWLEDGMENTS

Writing this book was an amazing opportunity to explore my own experience as an immigrant in the United States. Although I was a little older than María Emilia when I first arrived in this country, I too faced the same frustrations over my accent and not being able to understand people when I'd been studying English all my life! The food tasted so different, and it was very hard to have two winters in a row. Unlike María Emilia, I immigrated by myself and I didn't see my family for several years before some moved to the United States. I missed them every moment, and I miss them now.

This book is for the brave children—like my youngest brother, nieces, and nephews—who had to adjust to a new life in a foreign language.

This story wouldn't have been possible without the support and inspiration of my wonderful editor, Olivia Valcarce, a fellow Argentine to whom this book is dedicated. ¡Gracias!

Thank you to editor Aimee Friedman, a daughter of

immigrants too, and the whole team at Scholastic, including Jana Haussmann, Caroline Flanagan, Jennifer Rinaldi, Yaffa Jaskoll, Victoria Velez, Julia Eisler, Danielle Yadao, Kristin Standley, and everyone else who helps get my books in the hands of readers.

Linda Camacho, my superagent, thank you for believing in me and my stories.

Amigas queridas: Veeda, Aída, Amparo, Yuli, Romy, Olivia, and Las Musas for our retreat before the world went upside down!

To Mauricio Borba, Florencia Bellittieri, and Leticia Patrone Jessen, my first friends in the United States, my family. No sé qué hubiera hecho sin ustedes. ¡Los quiero!

Natalie Mickelson, Verónica Muñoz, and Rachel Seegmiller for making it possible for me to be a writer!

To my family in Argentina, Puerto Rico, and all over the United States, I love you.

Jeffrey, Julián, Magalí, Joaquín, Areli, and Valentino, everything is for you.

To the teachers, mentors, and librarians: For embracing

the children who arrive in this country whatever their circumstances and nurturing not only their minds, but also their hearts, thank you!

And to you, dear reader, always remember, those you love are never far.

Have you read all the wish books?

☐ *Clementine for Christmas* by Daphne Benedis-Grab

☐ *Carols and Crushes* by Natalie Blitt

☐ *Snow One Like You* by Natalie Blitt

☐ *Allie, First at Last* by Angela Cervantes

☐ *Gaby, Lost and Found* by Angela Cervantes

☐ *Lety Out Loud* by Angela Cervantes

☐ *Keep It Together, Keiko Carter* by Debbi Michiko Florence

☐ *Alpaca My Bags* by Jenny Goebel

☐ *Sit, Stay, Love* by J. J. Howard

☐ *Pugs and Kisses* by J. J. Howard

☐ *Pugs in a Blanket* by J. J. Howard

☐ *The Love Pug* by J. J. Howard

☐ *Girls Just Wanna Have Pugs* by J. J. Howard

☐ *The Boy Project* by Kami Kinard

☐ *Best Friend Next Door* by Carolyn Mackler

☐ *11 Birthdays* by Wendy Mass

☐ *Finally* by Wendy Mass

☐ *13 Gifts* by Wendy Mass

☐ *The Last Present* by Wendy Mass

☐ *Graceful* by Wendy Mass

☐ *Twice Upon a Time: Beauty and the Beast, the Only One Who Didn't Run Away* by Wendy Mass

☐ *Twice Upon a Time: Rapunzel, the One with All the Hair* by Wendy Mass

- [ ] *Twice Upon a Time: Robin Hood, the One Who Looked Good in Green* by Wendy Mass
- [ ] *Twice Upon a Time: Sleeping Beauty, the One Who Took the Really Long Nap* by Wendy Mass
- [ ] *Blizzard Besties* by Yamile Saied Méndez
- [ ] *Random Acts of Kittens* by Yamile Saied Méndez
- [ ] *Wish Upon a Stray* by Yamile Saied Méndez
- [ ] *Playing Cupid* by Jenny Meyerhoff
- [ ] *Cake Pop Crush* by Suzanne Nelson
- [ ] *Macarons at Midnight* by Suzanne Nelson
- [ ] *Hot Cocoa Hearts* by Suzanne Nelson
- [ ] *You're Bacon Me Crazy* by Suzanne Nelson
- [ ] *Donut Go Breaking My Heart* by Suzanne Nelson
- [ ] *Sundae My Prince Will Come* by Suzanne Nelson
- [ ] *I Only Have Pies for You* by Suzanne Nelson
- [ ] *Shake It Off* by Suzanne Nelson
- [ ] *Pumpkin Spice Up Your Life* by Suzanne Nelson
- [ ] *Confectionately Yours: Save the Cupcake!* by Lisa Papademetriou
- [ ] *My Secret Guide to Paris* by Lisa Schroeder
- [ ] *Sealed with a Secret* by Lisa Schroeder
- [ ] *Switched at Birthday* by Natalie Standiford
- [ ] *The Only Girl in School* by Natalie Standiford
- [ ] *Once Upon a Cruise* by Anna Staniszewski
- [ ] *Clique Here* by Anna Staniszewski
- [ ] *Deep Down Popular* by Phoebe Stone
- [ ] *Meow or Never* by Jazz Taylor
- [ ] *Revenge of the Flower Girls* by Jennifer Ziegler
- [ ] *Revenge of the Angels* by Jennifer Ziegler

Read the latest books!

 **shake it off**

 **pumpkin spice up your life**

 **TWICE UPON A TIME — Robin Hood — WANTED — The One Who Looked Good in Green — WENDY MASS**

 **angela cervantes — LETY OUT LOUD**

 **the love pug** — j.j. howard

 **girls just wanna have pugs** — j.j. howard

 **alpaca my bags** — Jenny Goebel

 **TAMILE SAIED MÉNDEZ — Random Acts of Kittens**

 **Wish UPON A Stray** — TAMILE SAIED MÉNDEZ

 **meow or never**

 **CLIQUE HERE**

 **Keep It Together, Keiko Carter** — DEBBI MICHIKO FLORENCE

SCHOLASTIC and associated logos are trademarks and/or registered trademarks of Scholastic Inc.

📖 **SCHOLASTIC**
scholastic.com/wish

WISHSUM21